Ulfat Idilbi was born in 191... She started writing in the 1940s and early in her career won a BBC prize for short stories in the Arab World. She has published five collections of short stories and a study of The Arabian Nights, and her first novel, *Sabriya: Damascus Bitter-sweet* has been dramatized for Syrian Television. *Grandfather's Tale* is her second novel. Ulfat Idilbi lives in Damascus and is the doyenne of Syrian women writers.

Peter Clark has translated many works from Arabic literature. He has also written biographical works on Marmaduke Pickthall and Wilfred Thesiger. He has had a distinguished career in the British Council, his last posting being in Damascus. He is at present Special Adviser to the Middle East and North Africa Department of the British Council.

By the same author

Sabriya: Damascus Bitter-sweet

Grandfather's Tale

ULFAT IDILBI

TRANSLATED FROM THE ARABIC BY PETER CLARK

Quartet Books

First published in Great Britain by Quartet Books Limited in 1998
A member of the Namara Group
27 Goodge Street
London W1P 2LD

Originally published in Arabic as Hikayat Jiddi by Dar Tlass Publishing,
Damascus, Syria 1991

ISBN 0 7043 8100 1

Phototypeset by F.S.H., London
Printed and bound in Great Britain by Cox & Wyman, Reading Berks

Grandfather's Tale

Translator's Foreword

Grandfather's Tale was first published by Dar Tlass Publishing House, Damascus, Syria in 1991. Its author, Ulfat Idilbi, was then seventy-nine years old. She has been writing short stories since the 1940s but this is only her second novel. Her first was translated and published by Quartet Books, with the title *Sabriya, Damascus Bitter-Sweet*, in 1995.

The story takes place in Daghestan, Damascus and the Hijaz. Islamic society binds these three diverse localities together. Until the First World War, Damascus was the setting-off point every year for thousands of pilgrims. It is an obligation for Muslims to perform the rites of the Pilgrimage to

Mecca at least once during their lives. Pilgrims used to flock to Damascus in the weeks before the Pilgrimage season and, as a safeguard against unsettled desert conditions, travelled together over the thousand-mile desert trek to the Hijaz. Pilgrims gathered in Damascus from greater Syria, from Turkey, from Bosnia, from the Caucasus and from the Muslim lands of Central Asia. The transnational cultural role played by Damascus as a great city of Islam is one of the basic themes of this novel.

Indeed it can be argued that *Grandfather's Tale* is an Islamic novel. People live within Islamic societies. The rituals of prayer five times a day, the idea that Allah is directly involved in the lives of His believers, the intense belief and sense of solidarity among Muslims are essential features of the world picture of the central characters of the novel.

A second remarkable feature of the novel is the background of the Daghestani resistance against the Russian expansion to the south in the middle of the nineteenth century. Wars in the Caucasus provided the background to some of the great Russian literature of that century. The Muslims of the mountains between the Black Sea and the Caspian Sea were an alien 'other' to Russians. To some extent this is still the case.

In the first part of the nineteenth century the mountains of Daghestan were peopled by dozens of tribes speaking different languages. The Islamic religion provided a rope of unity. The charismatic figure of Shaikh Shamil, a religious as well as a political hero, provided military leadership. A Caucasian Arabic has persisted as a lingua franca, used among different language groups, emphasizing over the years both a separation from Christian (or Communist) Russia and an affinity with the Islamic countries to the south.

Grandfather's Tale introduces Western readers to new angles and perspectives on the history of regions that are often overlooked. It is also a rattling good yarn.

In translating the novel I have received great help from Dr Mounawar al-Sayed of Damascus and from Theresa Clark. Both have read every word carefully, critically and constructively. Remaining errors and infelicities are my responsibility.

Peter Clark
Brighton, England
1998

3

Introduction

The great Daghestani poet Rasul Hamzatov, in the introduction to his priceless work *Daghestan My Country*, writes, addressing the book:

Before I embarked on creating you, I wanted to share my story with you.
How did you take shape in my mind?
How did I find a title for you?
Why did I write you?
What are the aims of my life?

When it was praiseworthy to follow the ways of older folk – and by older folk I mean not old in years but in the way of doing things, skilfully and with integrity – I used to enjoy telling the story of this novel before I started to write it. So, how did it take shape in my mind?

On my mother's side I belong to a Daghestani family that migrated from Daghestan to Damascus in the years after 1825 and still retains Daghestani as the family name. The migration of this family is a remarkable tale. There is as much delight as there is pain and tragedy.

I heard the story being told to the family from the time I first became aware of things. Parents used to tell it to their children and grandchildren, generation after generation, until my own time. I belong to the fifth generation. I often heard the story from my maternal grandmother, from my mother and from her brothers and sisters. Each of them used to tell a portion of the tale in their own particular style. I used, as a small child, to hear it so often from my mother or grandmother before going to sleep.

This is how it took shape in my mind.

I remember I once asked my Mother, as she was describing the fabulously high mountains of Daghestan in the way she had heard them described by her grandfather, 'Are the mountains of Daghestan as high as Jabal Qasyun?' We used to live at the foot of Qasyun, which I considered a giant among mountains.

Mother laughed and said, 'If another mountain of the same height were to be placed on top of

5

Jabal Qasyun it would still not be as high as the mountains of Daghestan.'

I was utterly amazed. My child's imagination was unable to picture such heights. From that time there developed in my mind a dream to visit the land of Daghestan and to see for myself those mighty mountains and yawning valleys.

Over the years this beautiful dream seemed to have died in the crannies of my mind, crowded out by other more vigorous dreams. Then I came upon Rasul Hamzatov's book and read it eagerly, impatiently. The old dream came again to my mind, just as a phoenix rises from the ashes.

I found that I knew a lot about the customs, the traditions and the nature of this land, for I had heard about them in my family. The Daghestani writer had recorded them in his book with great affection. In my case it was strange that it had not occurred to me, as a writer of fiction, to set down this uplifting story until I read Rasul Hamzatov's book, after which I felt a compulsion to write. I chose the title *Grandfather's Tale* because it resembles tales and myths rather than a modern story.

Why did I write it?

I wrote it because I found in it aspects of the human condition. I recorded it as a heroic tale about my forebear, Muhammad Jabali, who stepped aside from his own personal interests when he was an old man, sacrificing himself for the sake of his young wife.

I also recorded another act of heroism on the part of my great-grandfather, Salih, who was fated, as a small child of ten, to leave his homeland and his mother; but they never faded from his memory.

In his mind any reference to Daghestan called up an image of his mother. And any reference to his mother brought to mind his homeland of Daghestan. The two images merged and became one.

Is not the homeland the same as the mother and vice versa? My great-grandfather used to talk about them both to his children, to his grandchildren, to neighbours and to visitors for the rest of his life – and he lived to be over eighty years old.

When it became one of the aims of my life to write something really worthwhile I wrote this novel, and I wish to dedicate it to the young men and women of my country. I find in it examples of self-sacrifice, patriotism and filial duty.

I hope I have achieved some of what I have aspired to achieve.

Ulfat Idilbi

1

On the first evening of the month of Ramadan, Mother gathered us around the stove.

'During this sacred month,' she said, 'between the sunset prayer and the evening prayer, while your father goes off to recite the special Ramadan prayers, I'm going to tell you the story of how my grandfather migrated from Daghestan to Damascus. It's a delightful tale and I'm sure you're going to enjoy it.

'Every day I will tell you an instalment, just as Grandfather used to. He made us promise that we'd tell his story to our children and grandchildren so that it would remain alive in their minds. He reckoned it was too good a story to be forgotten. And here I am fulfilling his wish. Grandfather used to start his story from the point

*which had most affected him. He loved to talk about his
life and was a natural raconteur. Sometimes he would
embroider his tale with detail. At other times he would be
quite terse, as if to wind up one particular instalment.
This would make us eager for the next episode. I'm going
to start as he used to start, and I'll stop where he used to
stop. I heard his story so many times that I can remember
it all quite clearly. This is how Grandfather began...'*

I will never forget for as long as I live one
afternoon when I came home from school and
found Father pacing up and down in the courtyard
of our house. This was not his normal habit. He
smiled at me as if he had been waiting for me.

'Come, follow me to my room, Salih,' he said. 'I
have today a nice surprise for you.'

I ran after him. 'Are you arranging for Mother to
come here from Daghestan?' I asked eagerly.

He looked at me and his face clouded over.
'Why do you keep on about this?' he said. 'How
many times have I told you that your mother
cannot come to Damascus so long as her father is
not well enough to come too.'

'Two years have elapsed since we left Daghestan,'
I sighed. 'Isn't Grandfather getting any better?'

'Patience, my son. There is a time for everything.
Nothing happens without the permission of Allah
above.'

I held my tongue. This was always the way he

answered whenever I asked whether Mother would be coming to Damascus.

'What is the matter, my boy?' he said gently. 'Are you not going to ask about the nice surprise I have for you?'

'There could be no nicer surprise than Mother coming here,' I said quietly.

'Cheer up. There are some nice surprises that you may not have thought about. I have decided to go on the Pilgrimage this year, and I shall take you with me. We will go to the sacred house of Allah and you will be able to visit the tomb of the Prophet, on whom blessings and peace. Is that not a nice surprise? We will set off in two days' time, if Allah wills.'

I was lost for words and looked at him like a dumb idiot.

'I thought you would be overjoyed,' he said. 'I know that you take your religion very seriously. I have been to the souk today and have bought some new clothes for us both. I have also bought some cloth for the *ihram*, the special robe we wear in the Holy Places. And I have already arranged for an *'akkam* to get a *mahara* ready for us and to look after us on the journey.'

'I'm sorry, father, if I did not thank you immediately. I'm so taken aback I am tongue tied. But I must ask you: What's an *'akkam*? What's a *mahara*? These are strange words. What do they mean?'

11

'The *'akkam* is the man who leads your camel on the Pilgrimage and looks after it on the journey. And the *mahara* is the little wooden hut draped in the best brocade that is perched on the camel's back. It has enough room for two passengers and their baggage.

'But do not tell anyone else,' he added. 'I will announce it myself to the family after dinner this evening.'

After dinner he said to my two brothers in his firm calm voice, 'I have decided to go on the Pilgrimage this year, if Allah wills.'

'Can I come with you?' my elder brother, 'Abd al-Samad, asked. 'I'm old enough and I've not yet been on the Pilgrimage.'

'This year,' Father said, 'I am only going to take Salih. You can go next year with your brother, Ahmad, if Allah wills.'

My brothers said nothing. They did not argue with Father about anything he wanted to do.

'Abd al-Samad's wife then spoke, addressing me. 'From now on, my lad, we'll have to call you Hajj Salih.'

Everybody laughed at that.

I was unable to get to sleep that night. I kept thinking of Father and myself sitting in a small hut set on the camel's back, rocking from right to left. I had no idea how long the journey would take. I was slightly apprehensive, worried that Father, who was over eighty, might not be up to the rigours of the journey. But there was no way out. I would put my trust in Allah and be content with what He had ordained for me.

Next day at school I told my friends I was going to go on the Pilgrimage. Some of them envied me and I felt proud. Some were peeved that someone as young as I should have such an opportunity, for the journey was very costly.

The two days went by. We were in the middle of the month of Shawwal. We gathered our things and packed them into a trunk, and put some food that had been prepared for the journey into a basket.

We were up early. My brothers had already ordered a horse-cab that arrived at the house on time. They saw us off and we left the city just after the morning prayer. We reached a place called al-'Asali, from where the pilgrims departed together. There we met our 'akkam, a great giant of a man who inspired a feeling of assured confidence. It was his job to lead the camel and to look after us.

The place was swarming with people of all nations, features, colours and dress. We waited until the sanjaq arrived. This was the huge green silken banner, embroidered with silver and gold, that was borne on the camel that would be leading the Pilgrimage caravan. And the mahmal was like a small cupola draped in black velvet, also embroidered in silver and gold. This was placed on the back of a huge camel and inside it was the canopy that was being sent from the land of Syria to the holy Ka'ba in Mecca. The great caravan slowly came together. We heard music and a cannon was fired, heralding our departure. We set off, preceded by the *sanjaq*. Then followed the *mahmal* and after that the *takhtarawan*, a small litter also draped in a bright Damascene cloth. This was carried by two large mules. Inside sat the Emir of the Pilgrimage. After that came horses, camels with their *maharas* and, finally, people on foot. Our *'akkam* had sat us in our *mahara*, Father on one side and me on the other. To make up the balance the luggage and the provisions for the road were all on my side. I would never have imagined that this small *mahara* would have been big enough to carry us and our luggage and yet be so comfortable. There was on my side of the *mahara* a little window with a curtain that shielded us from the sun. I used to lift the curtain up and gaze at the surging sea of horses, camels with their *maharas* and humanity all tramping forward. What a sight!

Our journey was divided into stages. At the end of each stage the whole caravan would stop to enable pilgrims and their beasts to rest. The *'akkams* and the people who looked after the horses busied themselves putting up tents and creating a small city, lit up by flares – just as each tent was lit up by candles and lamps. Coffee-houses sprang up, with hubble-bubbles and drinks. Beasts were tethered at some distance from the tents and food was prepared.

I wandered around the camp and got to know

some of the other pilgrims. I would listen to their tales and then come back to where Father was sitting and relate to him what I had seen and heard. In the fullness of time the cannon would announce the striking of the camp. Tents would be packed up and the caravan would prepare to set off once more.

Neither Father nor I would complain of fatigue or illness as other pilgrims did. A lad of my age never gets tired. And Father, in spite of his age, enjoyed excellent health. He was strongly built as are all my fellow-citizens from the Caucasus mountains, who are renowned for their tough bodies and long lives.

It took us a whole month to reach the Enlightened City of Medina. Our *'akkam* led us to a good room which he regularly rented out to his clients. We left our things there and went on to the public baths, the *hammam*. I cannot remember ever being so content with a bath as I was after the rigours of the journey.

'Put your best clothes on, my son,' Father said, 'and make yourself spruce and tidy and we will go along and visit our noble Prophet.'

I did as I was told and we went to the mosque of the Prophet. I was overcome with awe as I gazed on at the priceless objects that adorned this holy shrine. We made two *rak'as* out of deference to the mosque and continued on our way to the tomb of the Prophet, on whom blessings and peace.

'Be on your best behaviour, my son,' said Father.

'Lower your gaze in reverence and respect. We are now in the presence of our noble Prophet Muhammad, son of 'Abdullah, the Seal of the Prophets and the Imam of the Messengers.'

Awe again possessed me as I approached the tomb of the Prophet and my eyes filled with tears as I recited the *fatiha*, the opening verse of the Qur'an, dedicating it to his eternal soul. I then became incapable of speech, unable to repeat the words Father was saying at the tomb. We turned to the tomb of the Khalifa Abu Bakr al-Siddiq, the first Caliph of Islam, with whom may Allah be content. We recited the *fatiha* to him too. We repeated the process at the tomb of the Khalifa 'Umar al-Khattab, the second Caliph of Islam, with whom may Allah be content. After that we started to recite the Qur'an until we were summoned to the noonday prayer by the *muezzin*.

After the prayers we returned to our room to have something to eat which our *'akkam* had prepared for us. We changed our clothes and went out to stroll around this friendly city with its gardens so green and its air so fresh. We passed three incomparably happy and agreeable days in the Enlightened City of Medina. Most of our time was spent in the mosque of the Prophet, on whom blessings and peace. We would pray and recite the Qur'an and then return to our room after the night prayer. We slept soundly and peacefully until the time for the dawn prayer

On the fourth day our caravan gathered itself again and we set off for Mecca the Venerable.

It was a very rough road, through rocky dull-grey mountains that rose on both sides of our rugged way.

'My son,' Father said, 'just imagine what hardships our noble Prophet had to put up with when he migrated, in the fulfilment of his great mission, from Mecca to Medina. He travelled along this very road on camelback, accompanied only by his friend Abu Bakr. Allah knows what physical dangers they confronted, with equanimity and steadfastness, as they strove to ennoble the word of Allah, may His cause prevail.'

Our caravan stopped at the town of Rabigh, where it was announced that we had entered the lands of Mecca the Venerable. Here pilgrims were obliged to make their ablutions and to put on the *ihram*. Father took the white sheets from his bag, handed two of them to me and showed me how to wrap one of them round my waist and to put the other over my left shoulder, tying the ends up under my right armpit and leaving the right shoulder bare. We remained at Rabigh longer than at other stops. We ate and we prayed, then the caravan reassembled and we resumed our journey to Mecca, reaching it four days later. The *'akkam* conducted us to another room he normally rented out to his clients. This room was not far from the sacred precinct. The landlord was at the door and greeted us cordially. Our room was spacious, light and clean. It had a sink by the door and a large pail full of water. We were able to perform our ablutions here whenever we wanted to.

We unpacked and washed. The *'akkam* took us to the souk to do some shopping and then to the sacred precinct.

What a fantastic place this was! I paused in silence and astonishment, contemplating for a moment its vastness. There in the middle was the *Ka'ba*, a huge lofty cube, adorned with a black velvet cloth that had been embroidered with gold and silver. People were thronging around it.

'Come, my son,' Father said. 'Let us pray two *rak'as* in honour of this ancient house of Allah. And after praying let us walk round it and take part in the ritual of running between Safa and Marwa in the manner of our Prophet, on whom blessings and peace.'

After praying we went round the *Ka'ba* seven times. The first time we were right in front of the black stone. We saluted it, walked round it and then saluted it again and walked round it again. And so on until we had done it seven whole times. After the seventh time we managed to make our way through the crowd and reach the black stone itself, which we kissed in the manner of our Prophet, on whom blessings and peace. Then on to the running place which was quite close to the sacred precinct.

'Run with the others and pray as they pray,'

Father told me. 'Leave me alone for a while. I will run at my own pace so as not to exhaust myself.'

'I don't want to leave your side, Father.'

'Do as you are told, without arguing,' he said sternly. 'That is best for you and it is best for me. When you have completed the ritual of running up and down seven times wait for me here.' And he pointed to a spot nearby.

I did as I was told. I ran up and down seven times, and found Father was still taking his time. He had run up and down only four times. I went off to look at the others as they performed this ritual – men, women, old, young. They ran up to one end of the course, then turned to face the direction of the *Ka'ba*. They recited a prayer specific to the occasion. They then came back, running briskly all the way. Seven times in one direction, seven times in the other. Allah knows, it was a sight I can never forget. When Father finished his running we went back to the sacred precinct by way of the well of Zamzam, where we drank until we had quenched our thirst. We then went to sit in a recess, reading the Qur'an until the *muezzin* summoned us to the night prayer. We joined the prayers and returned to our room.

We spent three days in Mecca before moving on to 'Arafat, a plain nineteen kilometres south of Mecca. Each day we would go to the space by the *Ka'ba* at the hour of the morning prayer; we circumambulated the *Ka'ba*; we read the Qur'an. When it was time to eat we went to the souk to buy whatever we felt like. Then we chose a corner where we would eat and go back to the sacred precinct to sit in one of the recesses. I would place a copy of the *Qur'an* in my lap and read it in a quiet voice. Father corrected my pronunciation and explained some of the verses.

'Your pronunciation of Arabic is better than mine, my son,' he said, 'because you learnt Arabic when you were young. It was of great benefit, your going to the Qur'anic school in Damascus.'

He said that because he had an accent when he spoke Arabic, an accent which he could never get rid of, even though he was well known as a scholar who had studied at the Azhar. And in Daghestan he used to teach Arabic, the Holy Qur'an and Islamic jurisprudence, and had been mufti in two neighbouring towns, Shakki and Shirvan.

On the morning before the start of the actual ritual of the Pilgrimage, we were sitting in the sacred precinct when some Daghestani pilgrims passed by. I noticed Father hiding his face as if he did not want them to see him. I was surprised at this, and could think of no explanation.

When they had moved on a little he pointed at them. 'Those pilgrims are from our lands, Salih,' he said. 'See that tall man with a black beard and a grey gown. Go up to him, my son, and tell him that you are Salih, son of Shaikh Muhammad Jabali. Ask him about your mother. Tell him to reassure her about you. If he or anyone else asks about me, do not draw attention to me under any circumstances. Tell them you do not know where I am at the moment or when I will return.'

'Who is this man who knows Mother?' I asked, looking at Father in surprise. 'Is he some relation of ours? And why don't you want to meet him? I saw you were avoiding him and his companions.'

Father gave no answer to my questions. 'I tell you,' he said firmly. 'Go at once before he gets swallowed up in the crush of pilgrims.'

Father's behaviour made me feel somehow suspicious. But it was not my habit to oppose him in any way. I do not know how I summoned up the courage to press him. 'I'm not going until you tell me who that man is.'

'Heaven defend us!' he said nervously but also loudly. 'When have you ever been so obstinate? When you come back I will explain everything to you. Get a move on now. He has almost left the sanctuary. We may lose him. Your mother will be so happy when he tells her about you and when she learns that I have brought you with me on the Pilgrimage.'

The words *your mother will be so happy* persuaded me. I ran after the man and caught up with him just before he left the precinct. I tugged at his gown. He turned round.

I spoke to him in the Daghestani tongue, the language of our home. 'I am Salih, son of Shaikh Muhammad Jabali.'

The man stared at me in astonishment. He opened his arms and clutched me to his chest, kissing me tenderly. He called his companions.

'Look at this fine young man,' he said. 'This is Salih, son of the Mufti Shaikh Muhammad Jabali.'

'Your mother, my boy,' he went on, turning to me, 'has never forgotten you. She is always talking about you. News of you filters through and she often dreams of you. She will be so happy when I tell her that I have seen you here in Mecca the Venerable, fulfilling the religious duty of the Pilgrimage.'

'Is my grandfather better?' I asked, getting the better of my tears. 'Will he be coming to Damascus with Mother? I so miss them both.'

There seemed to be some embarrassment in the man's eyes. It was as if he found what I was saying strange. His companions encircled me and asked me about Father, where he was and how he was.

In confusion I stammered a reply, distressed at having to tell a blatant lie. 'He is well, praise Allah. He is on the Pilgrimage, but I don't know where he is at the moment, nor when he'll be back.' I looked down, avoiding eye contact. They exchanged glances among themselves and whispered to each other, as if they sensed that Father did not wish to see them. They then said goodbye and went off, but they did not seem altogether happy.

I went back to Father and told him what they had said. I discerned no emotional reaction on his face.

For a while I said nothing and then asked him, 'Tell me, Father, who was that man who knows Mother so well and who embraced me with such affection, as if he was one of our closest relations?'

Father looked at me tenderly. 'Get up,' he said, 'and pray two *rak'as* to your Lord. Ask Him to give you steadfastness and strength, for I am going to tell you an amazing tale, my son, a tale which you will not enjoy hearing.'

'Grandfather suddenly stood up and said, "That is all for this evening. Good night, my children,"' Mother told us.

'We tried to cling on to him and get him to tell us what his father had told him. But he made no reply.'

2

On the second evening, Mother said, 'The following night Grandfather resumed his narrative.'

I believe we stopped last night with Father's words, 'I am going to tell you an amazing tale, my son, a tale which you will not enjoy hearing.'

When I heard these words I felt as if I was tumbling into an abyss. 'Has Mother died?' I asked anxiously, quietly.

Father smiled sardonically and turned to me. 'Are you daft?' he said. 'I sent you over to that man to reassure you about your mother and to reassure your mother about you. How can you wonder whether she is dead. How can it be possible for the dead to be reassured about the living? Say a prayer to your lord as I told you to. Then come back to me and I will tell you whatever you want.'

I did what he ordered me to do unquestioningly. I went off and stood at some distance from him, intent on my prayers. I made two *rak'as* to Allah on high. When I finished I raised my hands to heaven, asking Allah to give me strength and fortitude. I felt sure that I was about to receive a painful shock.

I went back to Father and looked him in the eye. There were heaps of questions in my mind. He was looking pensive and toying with his beard as if he was in great distress.

He finally looked up and gazed at me with compassion and tenderness. Then in a troubled voice he said, 'Do you know who that man was?'

'If I knew I wouldn't be asking you, Father.'

'He...he is...your mother's husband.'

I gasped. It was as if a mallet had come down hard on my head. I was passionately devoted to Mother. I missed her so much. I had been patiently waiting for her to come to Damascus.

'Have you gone out of your mind, Father?' I said in a tone I had never used with him before. 'What on earth are you talking about? Aren't *you* Mother's husband?'

'No, my son,' he replied firmly but gently. 'I am no longer your mother's husband. I divorced her before I came to Damascus.'

Shaking and swallowing my tears, I asked, 'You *divorced* her?!'

I was then silent for a moment while I absorbed the implications of the word.

'Why on earth did you divorce her?' I asked. 'Tell me, why did you do that? And why haven't you told me before? For two whole years you have let me savour the prospect of seeing her again. Whenever I asked about her you always told me that her father was ill and not well enough to travel, and that when he got better they would come to Damascus together. What a fool I was to believe you. How, how was it possible? It's perfectly clear...'

I buried my face in my hands and sobbed loudly and bitterly, not caring about anyone who was around.

'There is no strength and no power save in Allah the Sublime, the Glorious,' Father said. 'My reckoning is with Allah and his delegate. I concealed the matter from you, my son, because you were young. I was afraid to inflict an irreparable wound on you. But now you are older and are more aware of things I am happy to explain everything to you. But in spite of the fact that you are twelve years old it seems that you are not mature enough. You are still, as I see, a frail slip of a lad even though you seem tough and older than your years.

'Do you realize, Salih, that it is great shame for a Daghestani youth to cry like a woman? If you were now in Daghestan you would have a shining dagger hanging at your belt. You would be astride a fine colt. Together you would be cantering along the rocky roads among our lofty mountains. Or you would be galloping down to our hidden valleys with a skill that would continue to develop until you became as accomplished a horseman as your fellow Daghestanis. Their proficiency is celebrated throughout the whole wide world. They are courageous, venturesome and capable of restraining their feelings whatever ills the days may bring.

'No, no, you cannot be my son, so long as you are feeble-willed, weak, and weep like a woman! Listen to me, Salih. Even though we have migrated from our homeland it does not at all mean that we have forsaken our language, our customs or those traditions that we have inherited from our fathers and our grandfathers. Far from it. It is our duty to cherish them with the greatest care and to pass them on to our sons and our grandsons, until we are able one day to return to our homeland – and there is no doubt that, if Allah wills, we shall return. On our return we will not be strangers to our land or to our people.

'I therefore want you, my son, to be proud and resolute, as tough as the mountains of Daghestan. Or as we say,

As firm in your heart as the firmness of our
    silent hills;

As pure in your spirit as the purity of our
    dazzling white snow;
As liberal in your bounty as our bountiful
    springs.

'My son, a man without identity has no value.
He will continue to be a nobody whatever material
success attaches to him. The man to be despised is
the man who assumes an identity not his own. He
becomes a parasite on the community to which he
belongs. Rarely does the community accept him,
except when he is so outstanding that the
community can take pride in him. But seldom do
we find people so outstanding.'

I was enchanted by Father's words and from
them derived a renewed strength. I felt ten years
older as I sat listening to his words.

I was silent for a short while as I beheld new
horizons to my world opening up before me. I was
dazzled, almost transported.

Father's look full of loving concern eased my
anxiety and helped to restore a degree of emotional
equilibrium.

I took a handkerchief out of my pocket and
wiped the traces of tears from my face. I was feeling
better.

But I still looked at Father, seeking an explanation.
'You haven't told me why you divorced Mother. In
the name of the Prophet, what fault had she
committed that gave you the right to divorce her?'

'Allah forbid, my son, that your mother were to be guilty. In the name of Allah, she was a woman of purity and piety. It is I who was to blame. Yes, I was the guilty one in people's eyes. But in the eyes of my own soul I was acting justly, with fairness and goodness of heart and in control of a lively conscience. What matters more? People? Or my own soul? It is enough for me to have felt, since divorcing your mother, that I did indeed do the right thing.

'My son, I divorced your mother because I loved her as deeply, as purely and as profoundly as possible.'

I listened to him, my mouth wide open, in astonishment and disbelief. 'What you say, Father, is a complete riddle which I cannot unfathom. Are you saying that you divorced Mother because you loved Mother as deeply, as purely and as profoundly as possible? I must say, I don't follow your logic. I don't think I can ever understand it.'

Father smiled in a way that was both sardonic and sympathetic at the same time. 'You have now reached the age, my son, when you can understand what I am about to tell you. Your father only got where he did after the experiences of a long life. These have allowed me to rub along with people and to learn about their problems. Many people resort to their mufti to sort out their personal problems.

'You should know, my son, that the highest form

30

of love is when the lover strips away his own self-centredness and becomes devoted to his loved one, preferring her to himself and aiming to make her as happy as he can. I assure you that this is one of the most difficult things in the world. I put your mother before myself at the moment when I preferred her happiness to my own, when I put her interests before my own. I am completely aware of the fact that you do not believe a word of what I am saying. You may find it strange and illogical, but I do want to represent to you my own point of view. I will do my best to reach your young mind and to convince you.

'But it is time to eat. Let us go and eat whatever we can. Then we must come back here and pray. We can go round the *Ka'ba* again, and find a place to sit in some quiet corner away from other people. I will then tell you the story of my life with your mother from the day I married her to the day I decided to divorce her. It may be that you will be able to pardon your Father for the distress and suffering he has caused. Allah knows, I am completely aware how much you love your mother and how much she is devoted to you, and to have kept you apart is an unforgivable crime. But, my son, we cannot escape from the fate that Allah has decreed for us.'

I was actually keener to hear his story than to eat, for I was not in the slightest degree hungry. But I knew that it was pointless to argue with Father.

Nor was there anything to be gained by postponing the time for food. It may be that he was hungry. I followed him reluctantly and ate mechanically. We said our prayers and then found a quiet spot and sat down, facing each other. Father prepared himself to tell his story in detail. I prepared to listen to him with all my wits about me.

At this point Mother stopped and said, 'Grandfather would suddenly notice one of us yawning and he would say, "We've become sleepy, my children. Each one of us must now go to bed. Tomorrow we'll continue the story, if Allah wills."

'Then however much we pleaded he would refuse to go on. Instead he would repeat the words of The Arabian Nights, *"Morning overtook Scheherazade and she said no more."*

Mother stopped at the same point as her Grandfather. We knew that the session was over and that it was time for bed.

3

Next evening we were all gathered around the brazier and mother continued her story.

'I recall Grandfather asking us, "Can you remember where we reached yesterday?"

'"We reached the point where you both sat down in a quiet corner. Your father was about to tell you all about his life with your mother."

'"May Allah bless you, we had indeed."

'And he would resume where he had left off.'

'Life is not the bed of roses we would wish it to be, my son. All of a sudden, we may sometimes get hurt by unexpected blows. Your father, my son, was struck by such an unexpected misfortune. It caused him great sorrow.

'That was when my first wife died after an illness that lasted no more than three days. May Allah be merciful to her and judge her in the best light. She was a good and pious wife. She was several years younger than me. I had lived a happy life with her for over thirty years, during which time she had given me sons and daughters. They are all married and all lived independently in their own homes, just as I always wanted them to do.

'When their mother died each of my children wanted me to live with them. Failing that, they wanted to come and live with me in the old family house. But I completely rejected either idea.

'I preferred to stay by myself in my own house with my precious memories, and to devote myself to reading, praying and study. I was happy to have one servant who would come in and spend a few hours a day doing the housework. Things went on like this for several months without any change.

'Then one day I had a visit from a neighbour, your mother's father. He had been one of my students, and lived immediately next door.

'After talking about many matters he said, "My honourable mufti, I have come to beg a favour of you. I would like you to grant it, however difficult you may find it."

'I replied, with the purest of intentions, "I will not hesitate to do what you wish, good neighbour, regardless of the difficulty, provided it is within my power. You know where you stand with me."

'He rubbed his hands together, looked at the floor and said, "It is not right, sir, for you to live all by yourself at your age in this huge house without a wife to look after you and to see to your needs. It would be a great honour and pleasure, my honourable mufti, if you would accept my daughter Gul as your wife."

'I gasped at this bolt from the blue. I then burst out laughing and carried on laughing as he looked at me in astonishment.

'Are you out of your mind, man?' I eventually said. 'You want me to marry your daughter, Gul, who is young enough to be my granddaughter? To be sure it has been some time since I last saw her playing in our quarter as usual with her friends. Where is she now?"

'"Gul has grown into a young lady," he said. "She now helps her mother with the housework. But what of it, if you marry a young woman? Consider the example of the Prophet, on whom blessings and peace. Did he not marry our Lady Aisha when she was a young girl and he was over fifty? You told us about that yourself when you were teaching us about the life of the Prophet. But my daughter, by contrast, is no longer a girl. She's sixteen years old."

'I patted him on his shoulders and said with all courtesy, "But I am within reach of my seventies, as you know, and I am not the Prophet. Permit me to make my excuses for being unable to do what you would like me to do. But I am grateful to you for your concern."

'He was silent in spite of himself. He looked at me ruefully and then said as he was leaving, "No, no. I will not accept your apologies. I will leave you and you can reflect upon the matter. I will come back to you in due course."

'He then hastily left without waiting for my answer.

'One evening, several days later, there was a knock at the door. When I opened it I found your grandfather there and with him a sweet young girl of strong but slender build and of the most captivating beauty.

'I said to your grandfather as I looked at the girl, "Who is this sweet girl, Abu 'Uthman?"

'"This is my daughter, Gul," he said with a smile. "Do you not recognize her, my honourable mufti?"

'"As Allah wishes, as Allah wishes," I said in amazement. "Is this really Gul? It seems only the other day she was a small girl whom I would tease whenever I saw her playing outside. Do you remember, Gul, how I used to tug at your long plaits? You used to run away and I would chase after you, holding on to your plaits? You would whinny like a young foal."

'"I still remember that, my honourable mufti," she said, smiling coyly.

'"So what is your opinion now about what I said the other day?" your grandfather asked me.

'"Fear Allah, man, and drop the subject."

'"But it would be an honour and a pleasure for my daughter if you married her," he said, pointing at his daughter.

'I laughed mockingly at his words. "Is it true what this crazy father of yours says, Gul?" I asked the girl.

'She looked directly at me in a way I was not expecting. It was as if she was objecting to my words.

'"No, my honourable mufti," she said with a straightforward self-assurance. "My father is not crazy as you are suggesting. He knows that it would be a pleasure and an honour for me if I were to become your wife."

'I was tongue-tied and at a loss for a moment. Then I found myself saying, "I fear, my dear, that one day you would regret such haste."

'"Allah forbid, sir," her father said, "that my daughter were ever to regret marrying you. It would be a great honour to her to become the wife of the mufti. You can be sure that I did not bring her to you without consulting her. I am quite sure from her answer that she will be completely happy with such a marriage, one which will allow her to hold her head up high before her friends.

"My daughter, sir, is an intelligent and generous-hearted young lady. She is an excellent cook. She can bake bread and clean the house. She can also weave carpets and knit. She would be able to do many of these things in her spare time."

Father told me, 'It was as if, my son, I had been entranced by your mother's beauty, strength of character and virtue. In accordance with the decrees of Allah I found myself saying without any hesitation, "Let it be the bounty of Allah, then."

'Your grandfather then said, "Let us confirm this understanding by reciting the Fatiha together."

'And the three of us did just that.

'"I will arrange a wedding celebration, my honourable mufti," said your grandfather, "the like of which has not been seen in our land before."

'"Please, no, Abu 'Uthman, I beg you to spare me that. Do you want to make me the laughing-stock of the town? Me, having a wedding at my age as if I was one of the lads? No, no. Impossible.

'"I would ask you to keep the matter a secret for the time being, even from your closest relations, because I would like to surprise my children. I will not give them a chance to question our decision, but will present them with a *fait accompli*."

'"As you wish, sir."

'"Give me just one week, then. I will arrange a supper here at my own house to which I will invite my children and grandchildren, my daughters-in-law and my sons-in-law, as well as yourself, your wife and children. A few hours before the feast you must come with two witnesses and a shaikh who can ratify the wedding contract. That way everything will go smoothly."

'Your grandfather made no objection to my proposals and left me completely in charge.

'And so we arranged everything in the simplest manner possible.

'My marriage was a shock and a surprise to your two brothers, 'Abd al-Samad and Ahmad. But there was nothing they could do about it. They let me know that they accepted it but against their better judgement.

'As for your two sisters, Fatma and Zaynab, well, it pained me to see that there were tears of dismay in their eyes, though they said nothing. It was no doubt hard for them to accept this young girl in the place of their mother in the house. Every nook and cranny held some tender memory of her. It was as if I saw her in our midst reproving me with a glance. Tears welled up in m eyes too and I was unable to hold them back. I found myself saying to my daughters in some confusion and in a voice choked with tears, "Marriage is our kismet, our destiny. It is a decree from Allah Almighty. Do not condemn your father for being unable to flee from his fate."

'They then came to me, kissed my hand and said, "Allah forgive us, Father, if we were to begrudge you anything. We all want the best of happiness for you, the best that Allah has decreed."

'Your mother and her family were sitting in a corner of the room, quietly watching all that was going on. Quite spontaneously my two daughters went up to your mother, greeted her and offered their congratulations. Their brothers followed suit.

'We sat at the table in an atmosphere of friendship and mutual understanding. Everything seemed to be normal, with nothing more burdensome than I had anticipated. A load was removed from my mind when I saw my sons good-naturedly accepting the marriage.

'In this way, my son, your parents became man and wife. As Allah is my witness, I have not regretted it at all.

'Your mother was the perfect wife who looked after me with care and tenderness. I cannot recall that I had anything to hold against her.

'A year after the marriage Allah blessed us with you. Your mother and I were absolutely delighted. I do not think I was ever so devoted to any of my other children as I was to you. It was because you were a child of my old age, and it seems that whenever a man is old, he becomes more sentimental. He is weaker in dealing with emotion and simply submits. I made a fuss of you in a way I never made a fuss of my other children. I also felt quite at ease about your mother whenever I had to be away from home. I never worried about her being alone or about her becoming bored or restricted, for you had become everything to her. She would chat away to you and sing to you in her angelic voice. I felt that the house was dancing with joy. When you went to sleep she would sew or weave you some splendid clothes. She would show them to me and say, "How fine our son will be when he is bigger and can wear these clothes."

'Your mother seemed to me as if she herself was a small child again, playing with a doll. You were her favourite toy. I used to share with her such joy and happiness and it was as if I had shed decades off my life.'

'Grandfather screwed up his thick eyebrows,' Mother remembered. 'I can see him as if he were here now. He stretched out his hand and brought his watch with its golden chain out of his pocket. He looked at it and said, "Oh, my goodness, it is getting late, my children. Let us get to bed so we can wake up in time for the morning prayer."'

4

The following evening Mother took up the tale again, describing to us how happy her Grandfather was whenever he told his story. He would tell it to his children, his grandchildren, his family, friends and neighbours so many times that it became fixed in the minds of them all.

'I remember,' she said, 'how the next evening Grandfather seemed to be playing with his prayer-beads. At one moment he would be gazing into space, at another his eyes would glaze over as if he were reviewing his memories, or indeed as if he were reliving them. He then resumed his story...'

Allah made those days so sweet for us. For my first

ten years, life flowed smoothly. It was like the pure water of a spring in a green plain. Not a single blemish sullied its course.

When I was eight years old, Father started to teach me how to read and write Arabic. I found it extremely difficult, especially the grammar and syntax. If I fell short in learning some lesson, Father would sometimes be cross with me. At other times he could be very gentle.

'I want you to do your best,' he said, 'for I am training you to take my place one day and to become the mufti of this area. If Allah allows me to live long enough, I propose to send you to Egypt just as my father sent me. You can then complete your studies there at the Azhar University. You will come back to us as a famous man of learning.'

This spurred me on to do my utmost, and in turn pleased Father, who was ready to give me extra time for my studies.

'You're being hard on the lad,' Mother said one day. 'You're loading his brain with more than he can carry. Let him go outside and play for a while.'

'Listen to me, Umm Salih. I am an old man near the edge of my grave. I want to provide my son with as much knowledge as possible before I die, as much as I can give and as much as he can take. Knowledge is the most valuable legacy I can leave him.'

'May Allah lengthen the days of your life, my honourable mufti. May Allah never take you away from us,' Mother said.

'Can we exceed the bounds nature has set?' Father smiled. 'Every living thing expires, however far Allah may extend his life.'

That very year a revolt broke out in Daghestan against Imperial Russia. The Russians had tried to annex our small and poor country to their dominions, already vast and rich. The people of Daghestan rose to defend their lands to the death. Life became cheap in pursuit of this end. A man's homeland, the land of his fathers and his grandfathers, is like his honour and reputation. An offence against that territory is an offence against his dignity. Allah forfend that a Daghestani put up with that. Death on horseback, however disagreeable, is dearer to his heart than the humiliation that follows submission to a foreigner who has violated what does not belong to him.

Ferocious battles broke out between our people and the Russians. In spite of inferiority in both numbers and equipment, our men gained victory after victory. Daghestanis are fearless horsemen, practised in mountain warfare. They know the rough pathways, the gullies and the deep valleys. They would set up ambushes behind towering rocks, on passes with which only they were familiar. They were a match for the enemy army and were soon able to put them to flight, a defeated army suffering terrible losses to men and equipment. Only a handful of our men were martyred, bold adventurers who believed that their lives were not worth a handful of dust taken from the soil of their homeland.

The whole land of Daghestan erupted in a ferocious outburst of anger shared equally by men and women, old and young. The funeral rites of martyrs became like wedding feasts at which drums were beaten and maidens sang songs in praise of those who had died. The names of the writers of songs were hardly known, but songs in praise of martyrs were composed springing from the soul of the nation. Crowds would chant them as a spontaneous expression of their feelings. Mothers who had lost their children sang them, their heads held high, proud that they had offered their own flesh and blood for the sake of their country.

Mother interrupted herself to make the comment, 'As Grandfather spoke these words you could see the pride on his face as he recalled the heroism of his fellow-countrymen.'

Father told me all about the struggle. I would listen to him, entranced by his words. I can remember so many of the things he said. They have stayed in my mind ever since, though I was very young at the time. The funeral rites of the martyrs. The welcome given to the fighters when they came home after battle. Most people went out to greet them, singing and clapping.

On one occasion I went out with my mother's

brothers to one of these receptions. I was overcome by all that I saw. What pain and sorrow I felt when I saw one of the horsemen clasping to his chest the body of a martyr he carried in front of him on his own horse. The martyr's horse trailed along behind. The horseman was shouting, full of pride, glorifying his comrade's patriotic sacrifice. His declamation fired even the lukewarm. All were urged to join the ranks of the warriors.

I was even more affected when I learned that the body this man was embracing was that of his own son, his comrade at arms.

Mother told us: 'Grief fluttered on Grandfather's face as he paused for a moment. His eyes clouded over as if he was reviewing a painful memory. But he went on...'

The young man had been wounded during the battle, but he had carried on fighting in spite of the loss of blood. On the return home his life departed his body at the very edge of his home town. His father held on to the body.

The prolongation of this unequal struggle was tough, indeed without hope, in spite of our sensational victories. Ammunition began to run out. We lost horses at each encounter. We were unable to buy what we needed, for cash was becoming short as well. Stocks of food were being depleted. We feared the onset of famine if the war were to carry on much longer.

Father thought he would summon the shaikhs and learned men of the land to a conference during which they would examine the dire situation which, in spite of our victories, we found ourselves in. There was a speedy response to Father's call and the conference was held in one of the mosques. Representatives from the whole country attended. After a long discussion it was agreed that we should turn to the Ottoman Empire and seek support for our revolt in terms of weapons and cash. Was not the Ottoman Empire the protector of Islam? Its sultan the Caliph of all Muslims, the Servant of the Two Holy Places? And we, Muslims, were locked in battle against the Russian unbelievers who had committed aggression against us in order to annex our land to theirs. The Russians were also the enemies of the Ottoman Empire, so it would be quite fitting for them to give as much support as they could to our revolt.

The conference elected a delegation to go to Constantinople and call on Sultan Mahmud.

'They elected me as one of the delegation,' Father said. 'I did my best to excuse myself, for the journey to Constantinople was not an easy one for a man approaching eighty. But they would not accept my excuses. They insisted that I be part of the delegation, especially as the idea had originally come from me. I had no alternative but to answer the call of national duty and disregard the hardships.

'From then on, my son, the course of your

father's life was completely transformed. I had only myself to blame.

'You and your mother, Salih, went to live with your grandfather while I was away. I feared lest some ill befall you if my journey were to be prolonged and you were by yourselves in this huge house.'

'I remember that, Father,' I said. 'I also remember you gave Mother a bag full of cash. You told her not to ask any favours from anybody, either for herself or for me.'

'May Allah bless you. That is true, by Allah. You have an excellent memory, my boy.

'I felt a lump in my throat when I bade farewell to your mother,' he went on. 'It was a strange feeling. I had an uncanny premonition that I would not see her again. I will say nothing of the hardships we had to put up with on that long journey. Your old father found it particularly difficult. However, we reached Constantinople and, thanks to some elderly Circassian citizens, we managed to get an audience with Sultan Mahmud, Caliph of the Muslims and Servant of the Two Holy Places. The Sultan received us with more warmth than we had expected. When we presented our case to him he listened attentively. He gave his blessing to the revolt and encouraged us to continue to fight the Russian unbelievers, who were not only our enemies but also the enemies of the Ottoman Empire, which would be happy to bear a generous

49

proportion of the costs of the revolt. That is what the Sultan said.

'He ordered his secretary to write an official letter for us. He added his seal and signature. This was his *firman*. He handed it over to us and told us to present it to the Ottoman *vali* nearest to the Daghestan frontier. It requested him to supply us with cash, equipment and arms, indeed all support necessary.'

Father took a leather pouch from his breast pocket. He opened it and brought out the *firman* and spread it out. 'I am afraid of losing this document, my son. We may need it one day. That is why I carry it around with me wherever I go. If I die here you must take it from my breast pocket and place it in yours. Look after it to the best of your ability. It is very important.'

He then laid it before me and read aloud what it said, explaining the difficult parts.

Mother got up and fetched this very firman *and spread it out, telling us, 'Whoever wants to read it can read it tomorrow at leisure.'*

We all spoke at once.

'Why is this firman *still with you? Didn't the delegation present it to the Ottoman* vali?

'I will explain it all to you tomorrow evening, if Allah wills,' Mother replied, just as it was all explained to us by Grandfather.'

5

Mother resumed the following evening.

'Grandfather told us he asked his father the very question you asked last night...'

'Why do you still have this *firman* on you, father? Why didn't you present it to the Ottoman *vali* who was nearest to the Daghestani frontier?'

'How could we present it to him? We were arrested before we reached the *vali*'s lands.'

'Who arrested you?'

'We were arrested in the name of the Ottoman State itself, my son,' Father said with a sardonic smile, 'and on the orders of Sultan Mahmud. Each one of us was banished to a town that was as far away as possible from any of our comrades. I had the good fortune to be banished to Damascus, this most hospitable city. That is why the *firman* is still with me. They forgot to take it away.'

'Why did the Ottoman state behave in such a strange way?' I asked in amazement.

'To this day, I can find no convincing explanation for what they did. It may be that the Ottomans and the Russians, two mortal foes on either side of us, reached an understanding to crush our revolt in exchange for mutual concessions at our expense. I do not know. There is a nasty taste about it. Or it may be that some two-faced adviser went to warn the sultan, telling him that a successful revolt by a minor people against a major state might set a precedent for other revolts from other minorities. Within the Ottoman Empire there are many many minorities who are reluctant subjects of Ottoman rule. For this very reason, the revolt had to be crushed in its infancy whatever hidden advantages may have accrued.

'Consider, my son, how the Great Powers play around unchecked with small nations, how they violate treaties and tear up agreements. Conscience is dead. Vested interests turn a blind eye to such absolute right, and a nation can be wiped out.'

'Your words, Father, make me feel disgusted with the world.'

'You are still young, my son. You are innocent and know little of the affairs of this world of ours.

The more you learn about it the more you will feel disgust, but you will get used to it. You will have to make a distinction between good and evil. For the world is not without its good people even though they may be few in number. But do not surrender to despair.'

'What you say, Father, cheers me up and makes me feel better. But I would like to ask you how you were able to live in Damascus, alone and a stranger, for such a long time before we arrived from Daghestan.'

'It is as if somehow the sultan wanted to make amends for what he had done. To each one of the delegates he assigned a good salary from his own private funds. We received this on the first day of each month all through our exile. When Sultan Mahmud died, or rather when he was deposed, these payments stopped and we became paupers dependent on Allah in a strange land. But, Allah forbid, I have felt no sense at all of being a stranger in sweet-scented Damascus. I have fallen in love with this beautiful and friendly city which has opened its arms to me and taken me in. It is as if I am legitimately one of its own sons. It was not long before I had friends from among the scholars and men of religion whom I got to know in the mosques. They appreciated what I knew for what it was worth. They showed me sympathy after all I had gone through. They opened their hearts to me with love and care and made my exile comfortable.

They vied with each other in inviting us to their homes when the rest of you arrived from Daghestan. For soon after I arrived I had written to your brothers telling them what had happened. I asked them to sell up our goods and to join me here in Damascus. My Damascus friends made sure that these letters reached their destination through contacts, Syrian merchants, who travelled on business to Persia. There they had Persian friends who managed to pass on my letters through agents to Daghestan. My friends suggested that I write several letters: if one failed to get through, then a second or a third was bound to succeed. I followed this advice and the letters arrived in good time. I am indebted to those friends for their solicitude and for the excellent arrangements they made.

'I must now explain what happened about your mother. I can assure you I miss her terribly. I thought long and hard about what I should do, spending two whole nights with only snatches of sleep, working it all out.

'I was pulled in different directions. In the end I examined my conscience. Was I permitted, for the sake of my love for myself, to ill-treat this woman who had looked after me so well? She had given me ten years of her precious youth. For me they have been the sweetest years of my whole life. I was an old man, over eighty years of age. My end was near. If I were to require your mother to leave Daghestan and to come and join me, could I be sure when I died that my sons and their wives would treat her well? I knew how much ill will they had harboured towards her, and how they might have worked against her welfare. Damascus is far from Daghestan. How would a young woman like your mother, had she wanted to return to her land, how would she have been able to cope with travel through difficult country with a young son? It was my duty to rid myself of my own personal interests for the sake of my love for this great woman.

'I had to divorce Gul.

'The very sound of this word was terrible to my soul. But the sooner I divorced her the greater opportunity she would have of marrying somebody around her own age or a little older. Was it not enough for her to have been married for ten years to a man old enough to be her grandfather? Once I had made my mind up, my conscience was clear, especially as I was convinced that she would be guaranteed a better future without me than if she were to have remained my wife and become a widow in the prime of life.

'Your mother, my son, is beautiful and intelligent. She is young and has a good reputation. Many would wish to marry her.

'What can I say, my son? Tears poured down my cheeks as I wrote out the deed divorcing her.

'Do you realize that only twice in his life – in spite of trials and tribulations – has your father known the meaning of tears? Once on the day my first wife died, and again on the day I divorced my second wife.

'I sent a letter to your grandfather telling him what I have just told you, and I enclosed the divorce document. I then insisted on him sending you with your brothers. I did this because I thought if you stayed with your mother this would get in the way of her marrying again. I thought she would refuse any offer of marriage for your sake, so she could devote herself solely to you. This would not have been in her own interests.

'I begged your grandfather not to tell her about the divorce at first. He had to pretend to be ill and to persuade her that it would not be safe for her to come with my sons to Damascus. I asked him to tell her that he would travel with her when he was better. She would then be able to join her husband and her son. It was essential for you to travel with your brothers. I insisted on that.

'Your grandfather carried out my requests to the letter. Your mother was deceived. Only after you had set out did her father tell her the whole story.'

With trembling voice I said, 'Mother must have wept and wept when she suddenly heard that she had lost for ever both her husband and her son.'

'Do not look upon the gloomy side, my son. Why "for ever"? Is it ordained that we live in exile in flight from our homeland, for the rest of our lives? We live in difficult times which will inevitably pass. We will go back home. You will then be near your mother and will be able to go and see her whenever you wish.

'But if it is ordained, Allah forbid, that we do not return to our land, then my advice to you is that you never forget your mother. When you grow up and work and have your own resources, then you must put money aside until you have enough to travel to Daghestan and see your mother. She will be overjoyed to see you because you will never have forgotten her. I also advise you to do all in your power to bring her here to this Holy Land so she can perform the obligation of the Pilgrimage. A Daghestani woman's greatest desire is to bear the title of Hajja. And few are the women of Daghestan who have obtained this title which gives its bearer such honour and respect. For if the road from Daghestan to the Hijaz is hard for men, how much harder is it for women?

'I also advise you not to write to your mother. The exchange of letters would be a source of distress to you both. Letters may be delayed for some reason or other, or some misfortune may befall one of you and you may complain about your concerns to the other. All this would cause stress and anxiety and would add to the pain of separation.

'Now, my son, I would like to ask you one question. You must answer with complete honesty. Do you forgive your father for his treatment of your mother now that you know the reasons behind what he did?'

'Father,' I said, 'it is you who should forgive me for my doubting you. Doubt can be sinful. Now that you have explained the reasons for your treatment of Mother I realize that it was as a result of your caring for her, a result of your active conscience. All this led you to deny yourself for the sake of the one you love.

'I do not blame you, Father, but I do blame fate. We have both been fated, Mother and I, fated to be separated from each other for ever while we are both still alive, and young.'

'How many times must I tell you not to be pessimistic? Seek the forgiveness of Allah, boy. This is His decree which it is not for us to oppose. Hope for the best, my son, and you will find it. Who knows, we may return after a short time to our homeland and you will then be restored to the bosom of your mother and can rejoice in her company, even though she may be married to somebody other than your father. Her husband is a good man, a man of fine character.'

'You know him then, Father?'

'How can I not know him?' he said with a smile. 'It was I who selected him for your mother.'

I was baffled by these words. 'It was you who selected him for her? This is most extraordinary. How could that happen when you were in Damascus and she was in Daghestan?'

'Your grandfather is a good and pious man. Our relations were not shaken after my divorce of his daughter. He understood the reasons for it. He appreciated and admired my view and was persuaded that it was in his daughter's interests.

'One day I received a letter from him, telling me that two men had come forward offering marriage to her. He gave their names. I knew them both very well. He asked me for my opinion as to which of the two I would choose for her.

'I chuckled at this letter from your grandfather. It was as if he were asking me about the marriage of my own daughter, rather than about the marriage of a woman who had been my wife for ten years! But I did not fail him. I wrote back, telling him that the choice was neither mine nor his. It was up to Umm Salih herself. She was a woman of mature understanding, who knew what she wanted. But for her sake I hoped that her choice would fall on...and I named one of them. He was worthy of her. I knew him as a good man, a man of religion, a moral man.

'A month or so later a letter came from your grandfather in which he told me that his daughter had chosen the one I had preferred. Your grandfather thought he was righteous and well balanced, in spite of his youth. This letter told me that he would be travelling with a group of fellow-countrymen to the Holy Land on the Pilgrimage.

'It is for this reason, my son, that I have brought

you on the Pilgrimage in the hope that you might meet your mother's husband. I was confident that your heart would open up before you learnt that he was your stepfather. Now, if you are fated to go back to Daghestan, you will feel no sense of embarrassment on meeting him. You will have shaken off any prejudice by then. Similarly your mother will be reassured when he tells her about meeting you in this sacred precinct. All has passed as I had hoped and you have met with him.

'I have been talking to you for a long time. I am tired and thirsty. Let us go and get something to drink. We can then perform our ablutions before the call to afternoon prayer.'

We left the sacred precinct and went to the souk to buy two glasses of tamarind juice. We had a light meal and washed just as the *muezzin* was calling us to prayer. After prayers we went to our distant corner.

Father busied himself getting his Qur'an out. He always used to read it after praying.

'Father, I beg of you before you start your reading,' I said, 'there is one more thing I'd like to ask you.'

'Have you not finished asking questions for today?' he replied with some irritation. 'Ask whatever you wish and I will answer with complete franknesss, so long as it is your final question.'

'I would like to know what happened to the revolt in Daghestan. Is it still going on? I've heard you discussing it with my brothers but I didn't understand what it was all about.'

'I regret to have to say that it is still continuing.

'Why should you regret that it is still going on? I know you to be one of the strongest supporters of the revolt.'

'Your questions are very mature for your age,' he said uneasily. 'But I shall answer you none the less. I want to explain everything to you in order to enlighten you.

'I have come to the conclusion, my son, after a long life and a great deal of thought, that our revolt is bound to end in terrible failure in spite of all our victories. Our small impoverished country is not capable of withstanding the mighty Russian Empire without the backing of some great state whose interests coincide with ours. We have not succeeded in finding such a state. We will harvest nothing from revolts save the death of our youth, the orphaning of our children, the desolation of our land and the decay of our remaining wealth.'

'Have the other leaders not come to the same conclusion as you?'

'What can I tell you about human nature, my son?' he said, shaking his head almost in derision of my question. 'The tinsel triumphs of leadership and a love of command have seduced the souls of some people. You find them turning a blind eye to everything for the sake of gaining a few trifles for their followers. They tell lie after lie until they believe their own lies and it becomes difficult to persuade them. But, by Allah, if I had the slightest hope, my son, of putting an end to this revolt, I would not hesitate to travel to Daghestan incognito. It would not be difficult. I would be ready to call for a halt to the revolt and urge that terms be made with Russia. It may be that we could find a solution that would satisfy us and would satisfy them.

'What does Russia want from our land? It does not need more territory, for the country is already extremely vast. But they see that our land, with its lofty mountains and its deep valleys, forms a natural and secure frontier for them. If we were to reach an agreement with them to maintain together this frontier against any foreign aggression they would accept. We would stipulate that they must not interfere in our religious concerns and must leave us to run our own affairs in our own way. If they were to repudiate such an agreement it would then be our duty to launch a ferocious revolt at the risk of total devastation, because in such circumstances death becomes nobler and more honorable than a life of humiliation and servitude.

'But it is out of the question that our sons would listen to me, let alone be convinced by how I see things. Behind them are the leaders and their followers, young men who burn with enthusiasm. They would say that I had become enfeebled with advancing years, I had become helpless and lacking in spirit. Who knows? They may even accuse me of treason. Why should such an abominable accusation be of any concern to me? I do not shrink from offering myself as a sacrifice for the sake of my country so long as I could be sure that I would succeed. I have had the greatest difficulty persuading my own children, so how could I convince those who are unrelated to me? You therefore find that I am beyond despair and take refuge in silence. It is a sign of weak faith, but I pray to the Lord to guide the young people of my country to what is in their best interests.

'I wonder whether you have taken in all I have been saying, my boy?'

'Why not, Father? I'm no longer a child. I have taken in some of the verses of the Qur'an so why shouldn't I not have taken in what you have said?'

'You have a point there, my lad. Do you know, you have exhausted me with all these questions? Leave me to read what I can of the Qur'an. And go and look at the other pilgrims if you wish, or have a stroll around. It may be that Allah will grant some repose to my troubled breast. I may doze for a little here. But run off. You will find me at the time of sunset prayer in the usual place.'

Grandfather then got out his watch and said, "Oh my, half the night has gone. We have not been aware of the passing of time. I've forgotten myself; my tale has taken me way back to the days of my childhood and my youth, and I have failed to notice that you are getting drowsy. I may also have bored you.

'We all said, "No, we're not at all tired, Grandfather. We want you to carry on."

'"But I'm tired from talking, just as my father got weary when he told me all this. Remember, he was talking from soon after the end of noontime prayers right on to shortly before the sunset prayer. I hope, my children, that you will remember what I have told you and tell in turn your children and grandchildren, so they may know why their family moved from the Caucasus to the land of Syria. Get to your beds now, and good night!"'

6

'Next night Grandfather started with a question, "Has it not occurred to any of you to ask me how I spent the night after learning that Mother had been divorced by Father and had remarried? She was now living in Daghestan far far away. Perhaps the chance of seeing her may not have given me any comfort at all, even though I had been waiting impatiently for her to come to Damascus."

'I remember,' Mother said, 'I said one night to Grandfather, "I did think of asking you, Grandfather, but I didn't want to break your flow. I was hanging on your words, Allah knows, I put off my question till this evening."

'Grandfather said to me, "Allah inspired me to call you Najiba, meaning clever, and that is what you are

65

indeed, my girl. If you ask me this is how I would reply..."'

That night was for me a night of sorrows, as they say. In all the years of his life your grandfather cannot recall a more harrowing night. I feared that I would never see mother again for the rest of my life. I felt as if I had lost her for ever.

We climbed back into our beds after dinner and the night prayer. 'We must get to sleep early, to get a good rest and be up early,' Father said as he was putting the lamp out. 'Tomorrow is going to be a busy day, for we are obliged to carry out all the hajj rituals within three days.'

I made no reply. I felt acutely lonely when our small room was plunged into darkness. I closed my eyes and tried to sleep but it was impossible. It was as if I was only slowly beginning to absorb the meaning of my tragic fate. I sobbed silently. I did not want Father to hear me crying. I did not want him to feel any pain on my behalf. I was persuaded that he had done what he had done out of love for Mother and for the sake of her happiness. I lay there sobbing until I felt cross with myself. I felt as if I was suffocating and could no longer stay in my bed. So I slipped out very quietly and gently opened the door so as not to wake Father up. I went out into the alley. There was nobody about. The city was wrapped in strange silence. The moon overhead cast a wan light which banished something of the loneliness of the alley. By this slender light I made my way to a huge boulder and sat down, leaning back against it. I recalled Mother to mind in those happy days when I lay in her arms and first became aware of the world; and I recalled that day when we were parted from each other, neither of us aware that the separation might be permanent. Had we realized that, nobody would have been able to separate us.

Loving images flashed past me, one after the other. It was as if I were living them again during those moments. I saw myself in Mother's arms at the age of three as she was telling me a lovely story and I was toying with the long plaits that were always swinging to and fro on her breast. She would end the story with a lively song in her quiet yet moving voice, quiet because she did not want to disturb father, who was busy reading. She would go on rocking me until I was fast asleep. Then she would tuck me up and withdraw to her and father's room, opposite mine. She would leave the door open so she could hear me if I were to wake up.

I used to wake up early, get out of bed and run to my parents' room. I would slip into bed with them and with delight they would play and laugh with me. Then Mother would get up and prepare breakfast and I would stay with Father. He taught me some of the shorter chapters of the Qur'an and we would recite them together. I would soon have them committed to memory. What most upset me was when Father's friends came to visit. He would summon me and tell me to recite these chapters to them. They showed the greatest astonishment at my being able to recite them faultlessly. This pleased Father and made him proud of me.

When I was a little older and no longer able to sit on my mother's lap, I was unable to get to sleep unless I heard a story or a song. Mother would come and sit on my bed. I would place my head on her knee and play with her plaits, undoing them and tying them up again. She would tell me a story and then sing a song. If I started to yawn she would lower her voice until I was fast asleep. She would then gently place my head on the pillow and slip away to Father's room.

This all went on to the day of our separation. Can you conceive the pain of this separation?

Father taught me how to perform ritual ablutions and how to pray when I was six years old. When I reached my seventh year I mastered the art of praying and he would take me with him to the mosque, walking there and back. Father would then go on to his place of work. I used not to play in the street like other boys. I preferred to stay at Mother's side, following her around in our big house as if I was her shadow. We would sing and play, and I would try to help her with her housework.

And I was now sitting all alone in the street under the pale moonlight, whispering to Mother,

'You must have wept a lot, Mother, when the news of the divorce reached you, just as I am weeping now. I realize that our separation may go on for a long long time, and maybe for ever. To whom can you tell sweet tales and sing gentle songs, my dear young Mother?

'I wonder if your songs have become sad and now end in prolonged wails, like the keening of mourners?

'Have you forgotten about your son, Salih? You can forget people in two whole years. No, no, you have not forgotten me, dear sweet Mother. That's what the man said, the man who has married you. He told me that you talked about me all the time, and that news of me filtered through to you, and that you dreamt of me.

'I have no doubt about what people said about you. They will say that if there is a pretty divorced woman, there will be all sorts of gossip about her, however chaste and virtuous she may be. They will say bad things about her reputation and about the reputation of her son when he grows up if she doesn't get married again. But rest assured, the mufti divorced you only out of love for you. As he said when he wrote to your father, he divorced you so you could remarry before you got too old. People will have gathered round you when you were all alone and I was far away. You had to go along with what they wanted, poor dear Mother, in spite of yourself. You can be quite sure that I bear no resentment against you at all. Indeed I wish you every joy and happiness, from the bottom of my heart, just as Father does. But take care, dear mother. If you have sons, do not love them more than your son, Salih. I am your firstborn. No son or daughter can love you as I love you.

I carried on whispering to Mother, as if she was there before me in the light cast by the moon. I could see her in her blue dress which I liked so much, her long dark plaits hanging over her breasts as she glided up and down, flying, as it were, between heaven and earth. She came near me and then withdrew. She came near again, so close that I felt I could touch her. I stretched out my hand to do so but she gradually withdrew until she disappeared altogether in the clouds.

I then ceased my whispering. I was confused. I was looking up to the heavens, my eyes wide open, gazing at the never-ending emptiness. I felt glued to the ground, motionless. Suddenly I woke up from my confusion, glorified Allah and recited the verse, 'Say then, take refuge in the Lord of all people and chase Satan away from your mind.' I was afraid that Satan had appeared to me in my mother's form and that I had been afflicted by a touch of madness. I got up and went back to our room, opening the door quietly. Father was still fast asleep. I got back into my bed, carrying on my train of beautiful memories.

Mother then said to us, 'Grandfather suddenly fell silent, looked at each of us, one by one, and said, "Well, I can see that your eyes are bathed in tears. I am not telling you this story to make you sob, little ones. I tell it to you so you can remember it and tell it to your children just as I have told it to you. Do not worry about your grandfather. I can assure you that I did meet up with my mother but only after a long time, as you will hear. But now we are all tired. Let us go to sleep. Morning has overtaken Scheherazade and she has reached the end of her chapter."

'We all cried together, "No, no, Grandfather, we aren't at all sleepy. We can't go to sleep until we know how you met up with your mother again."

'"But I am very very tired."

'He got up and said, "After three or four more sessions I will tell you how I was reunited with my mother. That meeting was so moving, so precious to me."'

6

Mother said, 'Next evening Grandfather began by saying...'

I believe, my children, last night I stopped the story just as I was telling you how I went back to my bed to pursue sweet thoughts of my mother in our country, Daghestan. The loveliest memories that came to my mind that night were of those delightful winter evenings she and I spent together in her father's house, with her brothers and sisters. May Allah cherish those evenings. They were so precious to my heart. Since I left Daghestan, I have always held that image of her in my dreams.

When snow fell in Daghestan continuously over many days, it piled up everywhere and houses became half-buried. It became very difficult to open the door to go out, and our people used to stay at home, going out only when it was absolutely necessary and then with the greatest difficulty. We used to eat up the provisions that had been put aside for just such days.

During those long winter nights a deep gloom would hover over the house which Mother found hard to dispel however hard she tried. Father would be buried in his books and would not raise his head from them. Mother used to knit a shawl in silence and I would play with some doll Mother had made for me from bits of old clothes. An oppressive silence hung over us all. One evening, and this was one of many, Mother looked at me full of kindness and winked, nodding towards Father. I immediately understood what she was hinting at. I got up and went over to Father, rubbing against him like a friendly cat. He stroked my shoulders in an affectionate way and I plucked up courage.

'Will you permit Mother and me,' I ventured 'to go to Grandfather's house and spend the evening with him? I'm missing my uncles and aunts.'

He nodded in consent. 'Don't be late back,' he said.

It was easy for us to go to Grandfather's house without having to go out on to the road. Their house was next to ours and a small gate connected the adjoining enclosures. Most people used to visit their neighbours via these enclosures during the snowfalls.

Mother quickly put her shawl around her shoulders and dressed me in a thick coat. She lit a lamp and took down the key that hung on the kitchen wall. We went to the end of the kitchen and down two steps to a small area where there was a low door. Mother opened this door and the strong pungent smell of the breath and dung of the animals that were confined within the enclosure overwhelmed us. Mother raised the lamp and locked the door behind her. The animals peered at us, their eyes bright when the light fell on them, making them look like sparks that were scattered here and there. Father's old white steed whinnied as if to welcome us. We heard the bleating of the sheep and goats. The sheep dog sprang up from the other end of the enclosure and came towards us to sniff at us. He came with us as far as the gate that led to Grandfather's enclosure. Mother slipped the key into the lock and turned it. The gate opened on to an enclosure that was larger than ours. The dog retreated as if he knew he was at the end of his territory.

Mother closed the gate behind us and went up a few steps. She tapped at the door. Her younger brothers and sisters rushed forward and sang out, 'Here's Gul with Salih!' They closed the door behind us and buffeted us with kisses. One of them took my hand and we went to my grandparents' room. I kissed Grandmother's hand and she kissed me. I then ran to where I knew my place was, in Grandfather's arms. He hugged me and lifted me up on to his right knee. One uncle who was only a few months older than I was came and sat on his other knee. He then enfolded us in the woollen cloak he was wearing and we soon felt the warmth flow through us. After a few moments my younger aunts and uncles got up and went to another room. My young uncle and I joined them. Mother and her oldest brother were the only ones left with my grandparents. We played together, danced and sang songs. One uncle played some soulful notes on a woodwind instrument, the *mizmar*. Another beat a few rhythms on a small drum, and we just danced and danced till we were bathed in sweat in spite of the fierce cold.

Mother then came and called us. "Come on in," she said. "That's enough noise and play. Aren't you exhausted?"

We followed her at once without any argument for we knew what would be waiting for us. We went into the other room and found that Grandmother had in her lap a small tray with piles of dried dates, raisins, almonds and walnuts. She picked out a handful from each pile and put them into the pocket of each one of us. We then sat around the stove happily munching our share until they had all gone. Sometimes Grandmother used to cook for us sweetmeats made of flour and decorated with roasted almonds.

Grandfather always seemed to be merry. He would entertain us with stories and divert us with jokes and play with us. He would pull a plait or tweak an ear. He would pretend it was somebody else who had done it so that a dispute would break out. He would laugh a lot at this.

After a while he would look at Mother. 'You must get up and go back home, daughter,' he said. 'Your husband may be needing something.'

Mother got up at once. She took my hand, placed her shawl over her shoulders and said goodbye to her parents and to her brothers and sisters. She picked up the lamp and we went back to our own house the way we had come.

Another thing that delighted me was when the shepherd came each morning during the winter. He would open the far gate of the enclosure after digging away the snow that was blocking the door with a huge shovel. He would then take the animals out of the enclosure after cutting a way for them through the snow. He would leave the gate open to allow a change of air, then sweep the enclosure before bringing the animals back in again and putting down fodder and water for them. I would watch all this and play with the animals. When they had finished eating and drinking he led out the females and tied them up. He milked them skilfully and speedily. Many a time I tried to imitate him but I always failed. When a pail was filled with milk he carried it through to Mother who decanted it into a larger container and returned the pail to him. In the winter there was hardly enough milk to fill one pail. We drank it with our breakfast, sweetened with sugar or honey. But in the spring there was enough milk to fill all the pails in the kitchen. The milk kept Mother busy all day. She used to make cheese, strained yoghurt and purified buttermilk. She would put the milk in a skin receptacle specially designed for it and seal it up. She would then sit down and shake the skin. She would go on doing this for hours on end. Then she emptied it and gathered the solid lumps, placing them in a special storage vessel for the winter.

As I lay there in my bed in Mecca, a distressing memory from my childhood crept over me. It will be with me for as long as I live. It is the memory of the story of Umm Ayub and her son Ayub.

After a lot of pressure Father had agreed to respond to the invitation of some mountain villagers to spend some months in their village and to give them some religious education, teach them how to recite the Qur'an and to instruct them in the principles of the Arabic language and how to read and write it. We travelled to the village where the people had prepared a fine house for us. They did their best to do us honour and to provide us with every comfort. This was the way Daghestanis treated their guests.

I enjoyed myself immensely in this beautiful village. Houses were scattered over the mountain, from the lower slopes right up to the summit. I soon got to know the village lads and they quickly got to know me and were kind to me. I was the guest of the village and the son of the mufti who had become their teacher. When classes were over we played together and climbed up the mountain to the topmost house. We then raced down to the lower slopes. The steep slope made us run at great speed. I was always invigorated by this game. And when the sun was about to disappear we would stand on the lower slopes and wait for Ayub.

This Ayub was a horseman of outstanding courage, a skilful hunter, a tall handsome man. He rode a magnificent steed and to us lads of the village he appeared as one of the knights of legend. Each one of us had the ambition of becoming one day like Ayub, this superb hero. We would copy the proud way he walked. We would mount anything and ride as he rode, as if he and his mount were one unit.

Hunting was Ayub's favourite pastime. He would set off each morning on his steed and scour the hills and valleys. He hunted rabbits, gazelle and birds. He was open-handed and would provide anybody with what they wanted. Generous to a fault, he would put to one side what he and his mother needed and hand out the rest to family, neighbours and friends. We often benefited from his generosity. To know him was to love him.

On one occasion during a bitterly cold winter he was returning from hunting when he was caught up in a sudden fierce snowstorm and drifting snow blocked his path. He struggled hard and managed to get near his home. He knocked with his rifle at the door of a neighbour's house. The neighbour fetched other neighbours and everybody hurried to his assistance. They toiled to clear the snow and to bring him to his own house, for he was utterly exhausted. His mother came and wrapped him up in a woollen coat, and lit stoves and fires. He fell into a deep sleep from which he did not wake until the following morning. He had a high fever and a dry cough. Neighbours came to call on Umm Ayub, disregarding the storm and the drifting snow. In our Daghestani villages neighbours were like members of one family, my children. Each person brought something for Ayub, a remedy, some medicine, some food or some warm clothing that was suitable for an invalid like him. In spite of all this care and attention, Ayub's health went into a steady decline. On the morning of the fourth day Ayub died! He was in the prime of life. He left a huge gap in the hearts of all who had known him. His soul rose to its creator on a day when nature seemed to be particularly angry. It snowed and snowed without stopping for a single moment. The winds raged from all directions. It was as if they were mourning and keening for Ayub.

During such frightful storms it was not possible to bury the dead. It was our custom in those villages to wash the body, wrap it in a shroud and carry it out and place it on the roof under the snow. It would remain there until the weather improved and the storms had abated. The body would then be taken to the cemetery and put to rest in its final abode. Some neighbours volunteered to wash Ayub's body, enfold him in the shroud and carry him up to the roof. They then went off to their homes after saying a sad farewell to Umm Ayub. Three women stayed to condole with Umm Ayub, seeking to alleviate her distress.

In the middle of that night a youth from the village suddenly noticed a light on Umm Ayub's roof, moving from side to side. Somebody was moving about on the roof. This young man roused his father and brothers. He showed them what he had seen. What was this light on the roof of Umm Ayub's house? And how could anybody linger on the roof at this time of night and in such a storm?

'We must go to Umm Ayub's house, my boys,' the father said decisively, 'however tiresome it is, and find out what's behind this light. A neighbour has a claim in bad times more than in good.'

The father and his sons struggled to reach Umm Ayub's house at the foot of the mountain not far from theirs.

'Grandfather then said,' Mother remembered, '"Did I not

tell you, children, that neighbours in our land of Daghestan are just like members of the family?"'

The father and his sons knocked at the door of Umm Ayub's house but there was no answer. They then climbed on to the mountain behind the house until they were at roof level. One of them jumped on to the roof and found Umm Ayub sitting before the body of her son, wrapped up in a woollen shawl. She had a heavy stick with her and also a lamp which was melting the snow around it.

'What are you doing here on the roof, Umm Ayub?' the young man asked, 'in the middle of the night and in such a storm?"

'I took advantage of the women dropping off to sleep,' she said amid her sobs. 'When I was sure that they were sleeping heavily I came here to watch over Ayub's body.'

The young man called his father and brothers. They all climbed on to the roof. He told them what he had heard from Umm Ayub.

'Seek the protection of Allah and be content with His wisdom, Umm Ayub,' said the father. 'Does Ayub's body need to be watched over?'

'I heard once of a young girl who died during a storm,' she replied, wiping away her tears. 'Her family put the body on the roof until the storm calmed down so they could then bury her. The roof was like ours, right up against the mountain. When the storm was over all they could find of the body was the skeleton and two long plaits. She had been devoured by the wolves. I'm afraid they will come in the middle of the night and eat Ayub's body.'

She then burst into tears, the tears of a mother who has lost her child.

The father and his sons did all they could to persuade Umm Ayub to go back into the house, promising that they would take turns in guarding the body during the night.

The following morning the father sought the help of other neighbours. They all rallied around for the sake of the poor woman. They dug a grave for Ayub at the foot of the mountain not far from the house. They put him to rest there, disregarding the snow and storms. We, the lads of the village, looked after Ayub's grave, and put flowers and green branches on it each day. We also recited chapters of the Qur'an, dedicating them to the unsullied soul of Ayub.

'Grandfather stopped suddenly and said, "We have reached the end of our story for this evening, my children. Tomorrow's session will be long and pleasant."

'We went up to our beds, intensely looking forward to the following evening.'

8

The following evening, Mother said Grandfather started with the words...

Those recollections I spoke about last night kept running through my mind until I was overcome with great exhaustion. It seems that weariness and lack of sleep had caught up with me, for I had fallen asleep for an hour or a little more before I became aware of father shaking me to wake me up.

'Salih, Salih,' he said, 'get up, my boy. I have never known you to sleep so heavily before. Have you forgotten? We are going to Mina today and from there on to 'Arafat. It is time to get up and wash. I have done so already and there is still some water for you in the bucket; it is still warm.'

After washing we went to the sanctuary and prayed the dawn prayer. We put on our *ihrams* and walked round the *Ka'ba*.

Father had made an agreement with a man from Mecca to look after our interests. We found him there waiting for us at the tomb of Abraham. He greeted us; he too was wearing the *ihram*. We then left the sanctuary. The man led the way and prayed loudly a special prayer calling on Allah on High to pardon us for the sins we had committed and those we would commit in the future. We followed him, repeating what he said, until we arrived at Mina, feeling not at all tired, in spite of the long distance.

We spent a day and a night at Mina, praying constantly. After the sun rose we made our way to Mount 'Arafat. Our guide led the way among the many groups to a tent he had hired on our behalf. It was furnished with all the food and drink we needed. We rested awhile and prayed some *ruk'as* which brought us closer to Allah the Supreme. We then partook of some of the food provided. Towards sunset we left with the groups to pray behind the leader of the Pilgrimage. We heard first an eloquent sermon about the obligations and the rituals of the Pilgrimage and then combined the noon prayer with the afternoon prayer. When that was over the Mount 'Arafat stage of the Pilgrimage began.

I shall never forget the sense of overwhelming awe as I beheld hundreds of thousands of people, all wearing the *ihram*. It was as if they were naked. Their heads were bare. There was no difference between rich and poor, old or young, prince or pauper. All were facing Allah, may He be praised and elevated. All were devoted to Him, proclaiming the declaration of faith and calling out, 'Allahu Akbar,' 'God is greater,' and offering their submission to His will. Their voices could be heard as one great awe-inspiring chant.

'Allah responds, my boy,' Father said, 'on this blessed day to the prayers of His virtuous worshippers. Pray to your Lord for what you want and He will grant your prayer.'

I was so captivated by what I saw that I was not conscious of myself. I forgot about my own distress and felt that my soul was separated from my body and was flitting away into the distance as if it was in touch with the world of angels. Here I was actually standing in the hands of my Lord. The only words that were any longer on my lips were, 'Here I am at Your service, Allah, here I am at Your service. Here I am. You are the One and Only. Here I am. Praise and gratification is for You alone. You have no partner in Your Kingship.'

I said this in a trembling voice, raising my head high and stretching my hands upwards.

'Is it not inappropriate to make demands on my Lord, taking advantage of this most auspicious day?

'Is He not the One Who knows all, and has knowledge of all that is in people's hearts?'

I left the matter for Him so He could decree for me whatever He wished. I would be totally content with His decree.

How wise father was when he brought me on the Pilgrimage so that he could tell me of his divorcing of mother. Would I have accepted his story and been satisfied with his explanation if I had not been on the Pilgrimage?

I was feeling that I was close to the Lord of the Worlds. This feeling made the matter of the divorce much easier.

The huge crowd remained at 'Arafat, calling out the declaration of faith, crying, 'Allahu Akbar,' and beseeching Allah with all the prayers they could muster until the sun started to go down. At that moment people began to move away from 'Arafat and make their way towards Muzdalafa. There was a great crush and widespread confusion.

'Take my hand, my son,' Father said, 'so we do not become separated from each other.'

I clutched at his hand and we followed the man who had taken control of our affairs. He continued to offer up suitable prayers and we repeated what he said.

Father had made provision for everything, perhaps because he had already been on the Pilgrimage in his youth. He took two small cloth bags from his pocket. 'Take these two bags,' he said to me. 'One is for you and the other for me. Put some stones in them which we can throw at the three *jamaras*, the stone pillars that represent the Devil. For each *jamara* there should be seven stones. Make sure that each stone is about the size of a hazelnut. It does not matter if it is slightly bigger or smaller. We will have to throw them at the Devil in three places. They are quite near Mina and next to each other.'

'Shall we actually see the Devil, Father?'

'I did not expect such a question from you, Salih,' he said, turning to me. 'I thought you were more intelligent than to ask such a question,'

I tried to justify myself. 'I only wanted to get things clear in my head, Father. I would then understand what it was all about.'

Father looked at me compassionately. 'As far as I have been able to understand, my son, I consider the stoning to have a symbolic meaning only. It means the repudiation of the Devil that lurks in our souls waiting for a moment of weakness to tempt us. This repeated act of stoning is nothing more than a strengthening of our souls against the Devil, the eternal enemy of mankind, so that we give him no opportunity of leading us astray. Do you now understand the significance of the stoning of the Devil?'

'Yes, I understand now.'

Father patted me on the shoulder.

'Go off then and collect some stones.'

I collected the stones with great difficulty. Everybody else was bending down and picking up what stones they could find. Inevitably, there was much pushing and jostling. We went and performed the sunset prayers and later the evening prayers at the mosque close by.

We spent that night at Muzdalafa. After the dawn prayer we headed back to Mina. There we threw the stones – that is, we pelted them – at the Devil three times. After that we accompanied our guide to a place nearby and purchased two rams. We slaughtered them and left their carcasses there for the poor and needy. With that we completed the rituals of the Pilgrimage.

Father shaved his head entirely and cut off a lock of my hair from the front of my head. We made our way to a secluded place and removed our *ihrams* and put back on our ordinary clothes. We perfumed ourselves just as the Prophet had perfumed himself when he removed his *ihram*. We took our time going back to Mecca for Father was obviously tired. We went into the sanctuary and sat down by a wall to have a little rest. When it became less crowded around the *Ka'ba* we walked around it seven times. This was an additional ritual of the Pilgrimage. We then went to our room to get some more rest after the exertions of the last three days. It was quite clear that the effect on my aged father was greater than on me. But father was full of strength of mind. He made no complaint and never grumbled about the rigours he had endured.

Suddenly, a crier circling the shrine was heard announcing in a loud voice which reached our room: 'The Damascus caravan is to assemble tomorrow near the sanctuary, after the dawn prayer and after the final circumambulation of the *Ka'ba* for the return journey to the land of Syria; may those present inform those who are absent.' He repeated this over and over again.

We stayed in our room for a few hours. Then Father said, 'Let's get up, my son, wash and perform our ritual ablutions. We will go on to the souk and buy something to eat, and some presents. We will then go to the sanctuary to pray, read a little of the Qur'an and offer thanks to Allah Most High Who has conferred upon us the blessing of a visit to His time-hallowed house.'

We bought some silk fabrics for the women of the family and some prayer-beads for the men, plenty of dates, lots of incense, and water from the wells of Zamzam in sealed bottles.

We lingered in the sanctuary until the afternoon prayer and then bought something to eat and went back to our room.

Father suggested that before we went to sleep we pack our bags so that at first light, after the dawn prayer, we could go straight to the sanctuary to pray and make one final circumambulation of the *Ka'ba*.

I never saw the sanctuary so crowded as I did at dawn next morning. It swarmed with people, like a sea with waves foaming and crashing together, for nearly every single pilgrim had come to make a farewell circumambulation.

I observed the blissful satisfaction on the faces of each one of those who had completed the rituals of the Pilgrimage. Some had come from distant countries, in the hope that Allah would grant them, after all their efforts, pardon for the sins they had committed or would commit. They hoped He would be pleased with it all. They were utterly content with Him, completely at ease and confident that they, His repentant worshippers, would receive the pardon and mercy of Allah. In their faith, they were dedicated to Him.

It was not easy to go round the *Ka'ba* because of the throng of people. We finally left the sanctuary. I was profoundly moved. I cast a fearful farewell glance, praying to my Lord that He might permit me to visit it again with my beloved mother. Tears welled up in my eyes and coursed down my cheeks. We returned to our room in the narrow street not far away.

At the door we found the landlord with the guide who had escorted us from Damascus.

Father greeted them both with cordial warmth. The guide patted me on the shoulder. 'How goes it, young Hajj?' he asked. 'Congratulations on performing the Pilgrimage. It was all right, I trust?'

I gave him a smile, full of pride at the title of Hajj which I was hearing for the first time. I felt he was bestowing on me a grave dignity.

Father handed back the key of the room to the landlord, took out his purse and paid the rent, with a gratuity as a mark of his appreciation. The man thanked father for his generosity. Our guide went into the room, brought out our luggage and went ahead. We followed a short distance behind and soon found ourselves in the large square full of the pilgrims from Damascus.

The guide led us round to the front of our *mahara*, firmly fixed as it was on the back of a huge camel. The animal had lowered itself to the ground and was chewing its cud without a thought for what was going on around it. The guide came along with a small seat and placed it near the *mahara*. Father sat on that, brought out his rosary and began to tell his beads. I stood near him, gazing at the crowd of pilgrims converging from every direction, all looking somewhat weary. In about one hour everybody had assembled. A man called out to announce the departure of the Damascus pilgrim caravan, the drum was struck, people got up once more and mounted their horses and pack-animals and the caravan set off with cries of, 'Allahu Akbar,' and of the declaration of faith.

We mounted our *mahara*. The guide had already sorted out our luggage, putting most of it on my side. Father sat on the other side to balance the weight.

The Pilgrimage caravan moved off behind the

emir of the Pilgrimage who was sitting on his litter surrounded by guards seated on their gorgeous horses. The standard-bearer could be seen in front of us all, with the gold and green banner of the Pilgrimage.

The sun was beginning to go down over the mountains and valleys of Mecca. Gentle breezes blew from all sides. The weather was just right. We were fortunate because the Pilgrimage season this year fell in the middle of winter, so we did not suffer the intense heat of Mecca or the searing heat of hot winds on the journey.

From that day on, my children, your grandfather bore the title of Hajj, right up to this day.

Mother said, 'Grandfather got up and said, "Good night. We meet again tomorrow evening, if Allah wills."'

9

Mother said, 'The next night Grandfather started with the words...'

As far as I was concerned there was an enormous difference between the journey there and the journey back.

On the way there I felt I was as happy as I could be. I knew no tedium or weariness in spite of the length and rigours of the journey. Whenever it was time to eat, I ate with more appetite than usual. Whenever it was time to sleep, I slept the sleep of the dead. On that tiny *mahara* in which I could move only with the greatest difficulty, it was as if I was in a swing that rocked me forwards and backwards in rhythm with the pace of the camel. I was lulled into an agreeable deep sleep until I was roused by Father for the dawn prayer. I would wake up feeling energetic and happy and the whole caravan would stop. I jumped down with the guide's assistance before Father himself descended. We performed our ablutions and prayed with everybody else. I then wandered among the pilgrims. Everything would draw my astonishment and attention. I only went back to Father when it was time to set off again. I climbed back into the *mahara*, chattering to Father as I made myself comfortable. I told him about the things I had seen and heard. He laughed at my quips and comments, and rejoiced in my happiness.

But on the way back it was quite the opposite. As I was perched on the camel's back I felt as if I was in a prison-cell, face to face with my own tragedy. I could not get Mother out of my mind. I wondered whether she was happy in her marriage, or miserable at being separated from me. I would find myself withdrawn all the time, crushed in my spirits, preoccupied, unable to banish the bitterness of reality. I was weighed down by a yearning for Mother in a way I had never been before. It may be that in my heart of hearts I had the feeling that I would never see her again as long as I lived.

For all these reasons the nights seemed long and heavy. Sleep eluded me and wakefulness was unbearable in that uncomfortably narrow *mahara*.

Sometimes in those moonlit nights I tugged aside the curtain over the window at the side and gazed out at the vast emptiness of the unpeopled desert. I might catch a glimpse of Mother just as I had seen her in Mecca in a narrow street, as I had leant against the wall. Perhaps this vision of her tempered my painful yearning to some extent, but she never appeared. I turned my gaze back sadly from the vast expanse of nothingness. Despair surrounded me on all sides.

It was not for me to conceal my feelings from Father. He seriously tried to make things easier for me, and told me stories of the lives of the prophets and the trials they underwent, which they accepted uncomplainingly; how they put up steadfastly with the hardships imposed upon them by Allah Almighty to test their faith in Him and their attitude to His rules. If only I could take them as my model.

Disconcertingly, I said to Father, 'Do not exhaust yourself, Father. Your son is not a Prophet.'

Sometimes my attention would drift away from what he was saying, and he would be talking to himself. I nodded to him to give him the impression that I was taking in all he was saying, but he soon discovered I was not with him.

'May Allah give us strength,' he said, 'I do not know what is to be done with you.'

He then leant over and handed me the copy of

the Qur'an that never left his side.

'Take this and read what pleases you in it. There is nothing like the word of Allah to bestow calm and spiritual contentment on a sad and troubled mind.'

I took the book and read a few *suras*. I certainly felt a sense of peace and calm. I carried on reading until we reached the next stopping place – for prayer and for food.

This was my state of mind on the way back. The journey really seemed long, wearisome and boring. Every day seemed to be an eternity.

I started to lose weight because I was not eating or sleeping properly. How could I sleep with these anxieties hovering over me – anxieties that I could not shake off?

After putting up patiently with much discomfort we finally reached the outskirts of Damascus.

Father said gently to me, as if he was pleading with me, 'Listen, Salih, my son. Tomorrow we will be in Damascus, and the family, and maybe some friends and acquaintances, will come out to welcome us in the suburb of 'Asali. I would not like them to see you looking downcast or unwell. I hope you can do what I will ask of you.'

'I'll do as you bid, Father.'

He patted me on the shoulder. 'May Allah be pleased with you. At the next stage wash your face and hair with the help of the guide. Put on your best clothes and make them look as neat as you can. And use some perfume. When you see people coming to greet us smile at them and do not let depression show on your handsome face. Let it appear joyful. Show delight at this Pilgrimage which Allah has bestowed upon us as a blessing.'

'Don't worry, Father, I will try and be as you wish me to be.'

The next day we reached 'Asali shortly before the noonday prayer. The welcome was just as Father had said: my brothers, some friends and people we knew greeted us with warmth and affection. They kept saying, 'We trust Allah has accepted your Pilgrimage and blessed it.'

We got into some carriages and made our way to our house at Bab al–Barid, just by the Umayyad Mosque. We found more neighbours from the district there waiting for us at the door of our house. They welcomed us, congratulating us on having completed the Pilgrimage. My older brother, 'Abd al–Samad, invited everybody in for coffee and refreshments.

I left them and hurried inside to say hello to the rest of the family.

'Abd al–Samad's wife welcomed me back with enormous warmth. She hugged me to her bosom and kissed me. I could see tears in her eyes and realized she knew all about Mother's divorce. She burst into tears and we sobbed together. She sobbed and I sobbed. She caressed me and said in a voice trembling with genuine affection, 'Don't worry, my dear. I'll be a second mother to you. You're the same age as my boys, and as far as I'm concerned there's no difference between you and any of them. Put your trust in Allah, my Hajj, and we will certainly return to our homeland and you to your mother's arms.'

'You know Mother has married again? Perhaps she's forgotten about me,' I said in a sad tone.

She stroked my head and smiled through her tears, 'No, no, my dear. A mother never ever forgets her child. What does it matter if she has married again so long as she's in good health. When we go back to Daghestan, if Allah wills, you can visit her whenever you want to. Who on earth is capable of separating a mother from her son?'

I felt a bit better as I listened to her words, so full of honest good feeling. I felt the greatest need for somebody who could show sympathy and to whom I could pour out my heart. I brushed my tears aside and embraced my other sister-in-law and my nephews and nieces. I saw that they too were weeping as they listened to what we were saying.

The younger of my brothers called me. 'Come out here, Hajj Salih. Your friends have come to congratulate you.'

I went out and there were my friends, some of them fellow-students from school, who had come to welcome me. I sat with them in a corner of the house. They bombarded me with questions about everything. I answered them and told them about my feelings about the Two Holy Places. I described to them their beauty.

It seemed to me that they looked up to me with wonder. This made me feel proud of myself.

'Grandfather then interjected, "Don't be surprised by that, my children, and don't blame me. It's not in my nature to make a fuss of anybody however much he has been blessed. But it was quite natural for a boy of my age who had acquired the title of Hajj. It is a title that many adults long for, people who have not had the chance of going on the Pilgrimage."'

We spent three days receiving visitors. Father had so many friends – imams from the mosque, shaikhs and students of religion.

On the morning of the fourth day after our return we were having breakfast.

'Will you allow me, Father,' I said, 'to go to school today?'

'Of course, the time has come for you to go back. You have missed a lot of classes.'

'Abd al-Samad then said to Father, 'I would like to say something Father, relating to Salih.'

'Go ahead, my son.'

'I cannot see how school can benefit Salih more than it has already. He has become so good at Arabic, both reading and writing, that he doesn't need to study any more. But as for religion and interpretation of the Qu'ran, it would be worth while for him to study with the learned men of religion at the mosques instead.'

'That may be so, but what is he going to do with the rest of his time?'

'I'm told that there is a very good man who teaches arithmetic and the rudiments of book-keeping at his house for a reasonable fee. I have heard much praise of him. A lad of Salih's age, with his alertness and hard work, needs only one year's study, or perhaps a little more, to master the subject. Our shop is in great need of somebody to sort out our financial affairs.'

'What you say, 'Abd al-Samad, is absolutely right.' Father then turned to me. 'What do you think, Salih?' he asked.

'I agree, Father. I love arithmetic, learning it is enjoyable, but I would like to go back to school first, even if it's only for a week. I have missed my teachers and school-friends.'

'As you like – but only for one week. Your brother will then take you to this accounts teacher. May Allah prosper you, my son, and guide your way.'

Mother said, 'Grandfather stopped talking at this point of the story. He got up, saying, "Goodnight, my children."

'We replied all together, "And goodnight to you, Grandfather."'

10

Mother said, 'Grandfather started the next night saying...'

As I had expected I enjoyed the study of accounts, my children. After a few lessons the teacher discovered that I and another pupil had an outstanding aptitude for absorbing rapidly and easily whatever he taught. He then gave us private lessons from which we benefited even more.

After a year and a half the teacher gave us a test. My fellow-student and I did well in this and he gave us a certificate entitling us to practise commercial bookkeeping.

Can you believe, my children, that I was only fourteen years old? I remember the teacher telling 'Abd al-Samad as he handed over the certificate, 'Heaven be praised. In all my teaching days, I have never come across a pupil as young as your brother who has reached certificate level so soon. The other pupil was three years older and had already been studying.'

'Abd al-Samad smiled proudly at me and passed on what the teacher had said to Father. Nothing pleased father more than to hear of my success and of the praise I had received.

Next morning I went with my two brothers to the shop and started to sort out the accounts as I had been taught.

'We have decided to pay you as if you were not a member of the family,' 'Abd al-Samad said. 'This will be in addition to your share of the profits.'

I am sure this was at the prompting of my good father.

Each month I allocated a modest sum for my personal expenses and put aside what was left towards the expenses of travelling to Daghestan to see Mother. My longing to see her had not wavered for a moment in spite of my pre-occupation with study and then work.

Memories of her came flooding to me several times each day. As soon as I laid my head on the pillow to go to sleep those charming stories of hers came back to me, together with those enchanting songs that used to lull me to sleep when I was a small child.

I will not conceal from you, my children, that I derived a certain amount of gratification from having an income of my own. It alleviated that worry that marred my otherwise untroubled life.

Soon I had enough money to set out whenever I wanted to. Nobody could stand in the way of my travelling, not even Father. No longer was I dependent on anybody.

We used to have breakfast, early, as the sun rose, that is, just after dawn prayers. We would often chat about our affairs. This was the only time in the day when the whole family would be sitting around the table.

One morning Father said to my brothers, 'Do you still go riding to the foot of Jabal Qasyun on Friday mornings?'

'Yes, Father, we do,' 'Abd al-Samad replied. 'We love it. We'd love it if you came with us in the spring. The air is delightful up there, really splendid. From there Damascus seems to be surrounded by green on all sides. It lies in the lap of Jabal Qasyun. The view would remind you of some of the Daghestani towns lying at the foot of the mountains. But Jabal Qasyun is not as high as our mountains.'

'I know the area well. I frequently used to go there with friends who were imams and shaikhs of the religious schools. We went to visit the mosques and schools of Salihiya where they taught. When they had finished teaching and debating with their students, we would go off for a picnic, walking by the Yazid stream among the bushes of myrtle and the beds of violets. Our trip would start from the quarter known as 'Between the Schools' and go on until we reached the mosque of al-Afram at the foot of Jabal Qasyun. We would perform the afternoon prayer there, then have a rest before pressing on to the spot where the riding takes place. There would be friendly races among the horsemen. We loved to watch it all. It reminded me of the races the lads used to have back in Daghestan.' Father was silent for a while and then looked at my brothers. 'Do you know why I asked whether you went there?'

'Is it for us, Father, to fathom what goes on in people's minds?' said Ahmad.

Father looked at my brothers searchingly and chidingly. 'I wondered whether it had occurred to you to take Salih with you to teach him how to ride. If I were still able to ride, I would have excused you. But in the name of Allah, old age is a killer! I cannot imagine any Daghestani of Salih's age not being a skilful horseman. Do you not remember that I taught you both when you were much younger than Salih?'

'Abd al-Samad looked a bit confused.

'I had considered that, Father, but I thought that if we wait a little longer, until our own children are older, we will be able to teach them riding all together.'

'This is not a convincing argument,' Father said sternly. 'Why should it fall on Salih that he has to wait until your sons are older? Take him with you next Friday and start training him.'

'As you wish, Father.'

Father got up and went to his room. His tread was heavy but his body was as firm and upright as ever.

'On Friday, if Allah wills, you must come with us and we'll teach you how to ride as Father wishes,' 'Abd al-Samad said to me. 'You'll love this great sport. But do you have some trousers that are suitable for wearing for riding, or shall I buy you a pair?'

'I've got a pair. Actually I've already done some riding. I learnt how to from some friends whose family have a farm and breed horse. They have taken me there and I have learnt how to ride a bit. I was able to canter without being scared.'

'You smart lad! Why didn't you tell us this when Father was here? We would not have been blamed so much.'

'I was afraid Father might tell me off,' I smiled, 'because I didn't tell him I'd been doing it. I was afraid he might have forbidden me. I didn't realize he was so fond of horse-riding.'

Once I started riding with my brothers I used to long for Friday mornings. I looked forward to them day after day. After dawn prayers we would have breakfast and put on our Daghestani clothes, our *kalpaks* on our heads. We would go to the horse-market and hire three stallions. My brothers selected an older horse for me, one that was docile and would not be too frisky.

Within a few months I was an excellent rider. My brothers chose a young horse for me and soon I was bold enough to enter races with others of around my own age. Sometimes I won, sometimes I lost but I didn't have the courage to race against my brothers for a long time. They won every race they entered and became known as the champion racers of Damascus.

Once I overheard two Damascene riders talking as they were watching my brothers in a race. 'Those two Daghestani riders are superb,' said one. 'They seem to make their mounts fly like birds.'

'You too are a very good rider. Why don't you race them?' said the other.

The first man smiled, shook his head and said, 'Do you imagine, man, that I would fall into this trap of yours? You want to embarrass me and see me lose, because you have been unable to beat me, however hard you try. The Daghestanis, my good friend, have dazzled the Russians with their horsemanship. They continue to do so. You want us to triumph over them?'

I felt proud when I listened to these words. When I repeated them to Father, a cloud of sadness passed over his face.

'What troubles you have gone through, my Daghestan!' he sighed. 'How sorry I feel for your young horsemen who die to no avail.'

Mother finished her tale that evening with the words, 'Grandfather got up and a cloud of sadness passed over his face. He said quietly to us, "Goodnight."'

11

Mother said, 'Grandfather resumed his tale when we had gathered around him. He said...'

One day I noticed as we had breakfast that Father was unusually quiet. He ate very little. It seemed to me he had something serious on his mind.

When we had finished eating and were getting ready to go off to work, Father said in a deep voice that brooked no challenge, 'Sit down a moment. I want to say something.'

We all looked at him and he then surprised us by announcing, 'I have decided, if Allah wills, to travel to Cairo with some merchant friends in two days' time.'

'To Cairo?' we all stammered in amazement.

'Yes, to Cairo,' he laughed. 'You seem as surprised as if I had said I was going to travel to Never-Never Land. Cairo is not very far from Damascus.'

'Would Father let us know what has made him decide on this journey so suddenly?' 'Abd al-Samad asked.

'It is not such a sudden decision as you may suppose, my sons. I have been thinking about it for a long time. I decided that the time was right when I found some friends ready to go with me.

'The aim of my journey is this: I have some Egyptian friends who were among my comrades when I was a student. I understand that they now fill important positions in Cairo. Some are close to the Viceroy of Egypt, Muhammad 'Ali. I have asked them to arrange for me to have an audience with the Viceroy. I want to ask him to mediate on my behalf with the Ottoman authorities so that we can return to our homeland. I am certain that my friends will do all they can to secure such a favour. I know that they have an affection for me and that they have some influence. What would be of great distress to me, my sons, is to die in a foreign land and not be buried in the soil of Daghestan.

'I begin to think my hour is at hand. Everything has its appointed time.'

'Allah forbid that any harm befall you,' we all cried.

'Why should it keep its distance?' he smiled. 'It is

inevitable, it is the way of the world.'

'Father, let me go with you on this journey,' said 'Abd al-Samad. 'It's a tiring trip for someone of your age.'

'No, I do not need to be looked after by any of you,' Father said decisively. 'I am in good health, praise be to Allah. My mind is even better, and my friends will look after me if I need help as well as any one of you – that is, if I am in need of the care of anyone other than our Lord.'

'For ages,' said my brother, 'I have dreamt of going to Cairo. Please, Father, take me, let me travel with you.'

'You can go to Cairo whenever you want to, without having to look after me. But on this occasion I do not want any of you to come with me. Is that understood? The expense of travel is great these days. We need to look after our cash rather than spend it needlessly.' He then got up to go to his room. 'It is only for ten days and it will all go well, if Allah wills,' he said. 'We will undergo only what is ordained by Allah.'

When Father had retired, 'Abd al–Samad said, 'There is no power, no strength save in Allah. I don't think the journey is a good idea. But we cannot make him change his mind. Once he has decided on something he never goes back on his word.'

'We must all prayer to Allah that all goes well,' we said.

After Father set off gloom and sadness hovered over the household. We hardly spoke to each other about our thoughts and fears. Each one of us kept his misgivings to himself, unwilling to share them with others and believing that he alone was apprehensive about this journey.

Ten days passed without any news from Father. Our misgivings grew. Three more days went by. Then one of Father's friends who had gone with him to Cairo came to visit us between the sunset and night prayers, bearing news of Father's death.

This news had a devastating effect on us all. But we received it with apparent calm and fortitude, albeit suppressing our feelings in his presence. We were behaving as Father would have wished us to behave – in a manly way in every respect.

We were silent for a while. Then Father's friend suggested that we recite the Fatiha together, dedicating it to Father's memory.

We did as he proposed and then showered him with questions.

'How did Father die?'

'Did he fall ill from the fatigue of the journey?'

'Was he struck by a sudden illness?'

'Did he die in some fatal accident?'

'The journey had no effect on us at all. Your father did not fall ill. Nor was he in any accident. As soon as we got to Cairo he got in touch with his Egyptian friends. They were most cordial in their welcome and were delighted to see him. They did what they could to get him an audience with the Viceroy Muhammad 'Ali, who received him in a way befitting his dignity. But the Viceroy apologized for not getting involved with the Ottoman authorities on his behalf. Matters were extremely critical between the Viceroy and the Ottoman sultan currently, it seemed.

'Your father came back to us after that visit. He was downcast, heartbroken. He said to us, "I feel that my hour is at hand. It is not decreed, I believe, that I will be interred in the soil of my homeland, Daghestan. If I die here, dear friends, bury me in that land belonging to the Circassians that we have visited together. There I can at least be among some of the sons of my land and people."

'He then handed us the money he had on him and said, "I think this should be enough to cover the burial costs."

'We did all we could to put him at his ease, but to no avail. He would not eat with us that evening. He performed the ritual ablutions, prayed and retired early to bed. When we went to wake him for the dawn prayer we found that he was dead – may Allah have infinite mercy on his soul. He died, sad and distressed, we reckon. His departure was hard for us, for Allah had blessed our friend with generosity, loyalty and righteous feeling. We had the death announced from most of the mosques of Cairo. A huge crowd came to escort his body to the grave, and we buried him in the Circassian cemetery, in accordance with his request, and erected a fitting gravestone.'

He then handed 'Abd al-Samad a bag in which there was some money. 'This, my sons,' he said, 'is what was left of your father's money. His watch. His copy of the Qur'an. We distributed his clothes among the poor there. We thought you would have no need for them.

'This is life, my sons. May Allah permit his qualities to be passed on to the next generation. May He prosper you and give you steadfastness and comfort.'

'Abd al-Samad took the bag, the watch, the copy of the Qur'an. He thanked him profusely for everything he had done for us. We bade him farewell and he went on his way.

We went inside and gave the news to the womenfolk. They wept and struck at their faces. We joined them in their tears. Now we were alone we were able to give vent to our feelings.

Some time later I went to my own room and closed the door. The room seemed utterly deserted. Father and I used to sleep there. I looked at his empty bed. I went over to it and buried my head in the pillow. I burst into tears. The citadel on which I had depended, in disregard of my own interests, had collapsed. Oh, if only Mother were here now at my side. She would know how to console me and to soothe my sorrowful breast. I felt I had been orphaned a second time.

In the morning 'Abd al-Samad sent somebody to tell the mosque imams the news of Father's death in Cairo. They announced it from all the minarets of Damascus.

In the evening we invited a number of shaikhs with fine voices to recite the Qur'an at the house. We opened our front door wide. For three days we received mourners, men and women. The men we received outside. The women went inside to be received by the women of the household. We offered bitter coffee to everybody in accordance with Damascene traditions.

After three days 'Abd al-Samad, who had now taken over Father's place at the head of the table, said 'I propose going to Cairo next week to visit Father's grave.'

I nearly said, 'Take me with you. I too would like to visit Father's grave.' But my other brother beat me to it and offered to go.

'Who will look after the shop?' asked 'Adb al-Samad.

'Blessings fall on Salih,' Ahmad said. 'He is no longer a boy. He can manage the shop in every respect while we are away.'

'We won't be away for more than a week.'

There was no point in objecting, so, reluctantly, I held my tongue.

While my brothers were away I looked after the shop as efficiently as I could. When my brothers returned they gave me full credit, though I felt sad and utterly griefstricken. They told the rest of us about Father's grave and how they had found that it had been put up in a manner that was just right. 'Abd al-Samad suggested that the three of us go and call on those friends of Father's who had gone with him to Cairo to express our warmest thanks for all they had done for Father and for ourselves. It was a favour we would never forget.

12

Mother began next evening with the words, 'I remember Grandfather sighing before he took up his story the next night. Distress marked his features. He said...'

One month passed after Father's death during which time he was never out of my thoughts for a single moment. Whenever I went to my room to sleep I felt a terrible loneliness. I always looked straight at his bed and visualized him there, stretched out, his eyes closed. I could almost hear him breathing. For me, I had difficulty getting to sleep. I suffered from waves of insomnia during which I would toss and turn until I was utterly exhausted. Then a restless sleep would steal over me from which I would wake up time after time to a disturbing dream or a frightful nightmare. I would only be rescued from this torment by the voice of the *muezzin* as he called us to the dawn prayer. I would get up at once and go out to wash. I would then go to the Umayyad Mosque near our house and pray behind the imam. When I had finished I would sit in the mosque courtyard for a while and feel more at ease as I gazed at the spaciousness of the courtyard. This would cheer me up, however downcast I was. After some time I would go back home for breakfast with the rest of the family. Then on to the shop near by to work.

One morning 'Abd al-Samad's wife called me to her room. She seemed embarrassed. 'My dear, do you think your room is rather big for you?'

'Yes, certainly. I have wanted to tell you that myself.'

'You are always so good and reasonable.'

What an ass I am, I thought. Would it not have been better to have volunteered first? It isn't right for me to have this huge room to myself while my eldest brother and his wife sleep in a smaller room.

She went on, 'The children are getting bigger. Their room is too small and it has become hard for two of them to sleep in the same bed. I plan to move two beds for the boys into our room, and to leave the four girls in their room. If you would like to sleep in the same room as your nephews I can

120

move your bed into their room. It's big enough for three beds. If you prefer to sleep alone I can get the cubby-hole by the stairs ready for you. It's big enough for you and your possessions.'

I was surprised for I had not thought of this solution at all. I thought they would have moved me into the room vacated by 'Abd al-Samad and his wife. I was slow in answering her, for there was no point in putting up any opposition; there was no doubt that the matter had already been settled. I said, a little peevishly, 'I prefer sleeping by myself so I will not be disturbed or disturb others.'

I then left her, wondering what things had come to. After having slept in the biggest and most spacious room in the house I was now going to sleep in a shoe cupboard, the meanest and ugliest room in the house. May Allah have mercy on you, Father, I thought. I don't know what injustice they will inflict on me next now you are gone. But what was I to do? I had no alternative but to accept the *fait accompli* with grace.

When I came home that evening I went straight up to the cubby-hole without saying a word to anybody. My bed had already been moved there. Beside it they had put the small trunk into which I had crammed all my belongings. A chair was squeezed into the space the other side of the bed against the wall. I felt like opening the door and violently throwing the chair out into the hallway in protest, but I curbed my impatience and looked around the cubby-hole. There was just eighteen inches between the bed and the wall. That wall seemed to bear down on my chest. The room had no window, only a skylight above the door through which a faint gleam penetrated. I sat on the edge of the bed and burst into tears. After a short while I calmed down and tried to examine the situation a little more positively.

What else could my sister-in-law do when the children were not big enough for two beds and I was the only one in the household to have a bedroom to myself. It was up to me to keep quiet and accept the changed circumstances.

The days went by without anything particular happening. The only happiness or amusement I had was on one day in the week – Friday – when I would go riding with my brothers in Salihiya. There I used to meet up with my very good friends, Qasim and Sa'id whom I had got to know at school. It was in their orchards that I had first learnt how to ride. I used to ask my brothers to permit me to spend the whole day in the orchards. Sometimes we would climb trees and pick whatever fruit we liked. When we got hot we would strip off and swim in the Yazid stream which flowed by at the end of the orchard, pure and purling. Abu Qasim al-Salihani, my friends' father, was the shaikh of the orchard-owners of Salihiya. He was an agreeable, good-hearted merry man. He loved me as if I was one of his own children. I revered him.

The days started to go by quickly. I was not aware of the passage of time for one day was very like another. Before I knew it, I had reached the age of eighteen. I was taller than my brothers and I sported a thick black moustache. More important than all this was the fact that I had saved twenty-five golden sovereigns over the previous four years from my salary and my share of the shop's profits. I kept the savings in a brown leather belt which I wore under my clothes so I would always know that they were safe. This sum was enough for me to travel to Daghestan and back and to buy valuable presents for mother and my aunts and uncles. I decided I would surprise my brothers by announcing my intention at the beginning of the coming summer. None of them would divert me from my objective so long as I had my money with me. I had no need of anybody. My golden dream would be realized. I indulged in sweet dreams and no longer felt upset about the humiliation of the cubby-hole.

One Friday came when I went riding with my brothers and met my friends, Qasim and Sa'id. Then I went with them to their orchards as was our habit for another delightful day.

Their father, Abu Qasim, greeted me with great warmth. 'You've come just at the right time, my son,' he said. 'Perhaps Lady Luck is giving you this time one of her rare sweet smiles. It's the chance of a lifetime. There may not be such a good chance again, so take care you don't let this one slip by.'

'What are you talking about, uncle?' I asked. 'You've aroused my interest. Tell me more, by Allah.'

'Listen to me, my lad. There is a sale today here in Salihiya, not far from this orchard. A house going very cheaply. In all my life I have not seen a more attractive property. What do you think of the idea of our buying it for you?'

I burst out laughing.

'May Allah forgive you, Uncle Abu Qasim. Do you imagine I've got enough money to buy fine houses?'

'Have you not told me that you have twenty-five golden sovereigns, enough to take you to your land of Daghestan? Daghestan is still there. Rest assured, it won't go away and your mother will still, if Allah wills, be there. She's not a frail old lady. But this house is all ready now and will not be available for long. If I weren't obliged to live in this orchard with my sons and to supervise the peasants' work – and our livelihood depends upon it – I would raise a loan and buy the house myself. The owner would be quite happy. He's a Christian and my friend. I know he's a fine and honourable man and he's selling this property at a third of its value – for just forty golden sovereigns. The man has got to travel to America this week, or within the next few days to be precise. His wife and children have gone ahead of him to Beirut to reserve a place on the ship after selling everything apart from this house. It's been up for sale for over a month, but nobody has made an offer. The people of Salihiya are not well-off and don't have the ready cash to buy large houses, and the people of Damascus find Salihiya too distant a suburb and don't want to live there. Come and let's have a look at it.'

'What's the point of seeing it when I have no wish to buy it? Anyway, I don't have enough money.'

'What have you to lose? It's nice just to look at the house. Come along. You won't regret it, if Allah wills.'

Out of respect for him, I gave in to his wishes.

The house was not very far from Abu Qasim's orchard. We knocked at the door and a respectable middle-aged gentleman opened it. His appearance gave every indication of mild-mannered fine breeding. He smiled at us in welcome.

'I've brought you a purchaser, Khawaja Yusuf, if Allah wills,' said Abu Qasim.

I thought he was in jest. When we came out of the entrance hall and into a courtyard I stood in amazement, entranced. I had never seen a grander house. To tell you the truth, from that first moment I fell in love with the house. It was like paradise with rivers running through.

The courtyard was extensive and rectangular, and inlaid with black stones and marble of a rose colour. It was paved in a way that was technically superb. In the middle was a bubbling fountain, fashioned also in fine marble. The courtyard had a *liwan* to the right of which were two small rooms, to the left two small rooms and a kitchen. It was springtime and the roses were out, as well as gillyflower, lilac and elegant marvel-of-Peru in flowerbeds around the fountain. There was jasmine overhead, yellow and white violets as well as creepers on the walls. The courtyard overlooked a large garden which you reached by some steps of rose-coloured marble. The Yazid stream divided the garden into two parts joined by a narrow bridge. In front of the bridge there rose a huge water-wheel that conducted water to the fountain and also to the kitchen. The gentle creak from the water-wheel mingled with the trickling of the water as it cascaded from the water-wheel and with the chirping of the birds. It was all a wonderful symphony to Mother Nature. In the garden there were trees of plum, apricot, peach and apple. Spring had adorned them with fragrant white blossom. In the name of Allah, it was as if a bride was looking at her groom who was about to unveil her. A trellis of vine hung over the stream. At the far end of the garden in the middle of a wall was a low door. Khawaja Yusuf pointed to the gate. 'That door,' he said, 'leads to the outside garden.'

I was astonished when I realized that there was another garden. Khawaja Yusuf took a key from his pocket and opened the low door. There before us was a garden that was bigger than the inside garden. It was planted with citrus fruit, walnut and hazelnut trees. We then went back up to the outhouse which was smaller than the main house and not quite so elegant. He went off to prepare some coffee for us.

Abu Qasim whispered in my ear, 'Don't lose this chance, my son. I can lend you fifteen golden sovereigns. I've brought all my spare cash with me, which is no more than twenty sovereigns. If you don't want to keep this house you can sell it at your leisure at double the price. Each of us can take our share of the profit. If you wish to keep it, and I hope this is what you will do, you can pay off my loan little by little. Take as much time as you wish.

'I will be surer of my cash,' he laughed, 'if it is in trust to you rather than in the till, in danger of being stolen at any time. When we've had some coffee we'll draw up a deed of sale and in the morning we'll go with Khawaja Yusuf and register the purchase at the Lands Department.'

'No, no, uncle, I beg of you. I cannot sign any deed of sale until I have consulted my brothers. They'll be angry with me if I don't seek their advice on a matter of such importance. I am very anxious to get their approval.'

'Take care what you do, my dear Salih,' Abu Qasim insisted. 'Your brothers may not agree to the purchase for some reason or other. In being obliged to keep their goodwill you may have to withdraw from the deal and this would not be at all in your interests. You would regret it most profoundly. You

127

are now a grown man, legally capable of looking after your own affairs as you see fit. What will happen? Your brothers will be cross for a while. Then it won't be long before things are back to normal. But I can assure you that your brothers will be very happy for you when they see this property which is like paradise.'

After drinking coffee we drew up a deed and agreed that we would go the next morning to register the purchase. Abu Qasim looked around and then said to the owner of the house, 'Khawaja Yusuf, aren't you going to let us have these few sticks of furniture as a present instead of as a purchase?'

The other man laughed. 'May God forgive you, Abu Qasim. Do you call these magnificent thrones, benches, trunks and chairs, finely carved from the best walnut-tree wood by the most skilled carpenters, "sticks of furniture"? I have known you as a successful cultivator, but not as a sophisticated merchant. In God's name, but for the fact that transporting them to America would cost a lot of money I would not be leaving them behind at all. I did arrange for an agent to bring some customers this morning. We have heard the call for the noon prayer and they have not yet come.'

'There's nobody more dishonest than these agents,' said Abu Qasim. 'I wouldn't have anything to do with them. To pacify you, we'll pay you two sovereigns for them. This is as much as we can pay.

What do you think?'

Khawaja Yusuf turned and said, 'Let it be with the blessings of God.'

Abu Qasim put his hand in his pocket and brought out a bag in which he kept all his cash. He counted out seventeen golden sovereigns and handed them over. I also loosened my belt and brought out my own cash, twenty-five golden sovereigns, and paid them out to him. He wrote us a receipt which he gave to Abu Qasim and handed me the key of the house.

'A thousand congratulations, my son,' he said affably. 'I am very happy that this house, which has been so dear to me, passes into the hands of a fine young man like yourself who appreciates beauty and good taste. Look after its bushes, my son, and its blooms. I have tended them with the help of God and looked after them as I have looked after my own children.' And his eyes became filled with tears.

I too nearly wept as I was listening to him. It was as if the key that was still in my hand was waking me up from a beautiful dream to disagreeable reality. I stood in silence, thinking that I had betrayed Mother in preferring this house to going to visit her. I had failed in my duty towards my brothers in buying this house without consulting them. This was no small matter as far as they were concerned. And I was in debt. I did not know how I was going to sort my affairs out. What a mess I'd got myself in, thanks to Abu Qasim, even though he had the best of intentions.

Mother said, 'When Grandfather reached this point he got up. We pleaded, 'Tell us, Grandfather, in just two words. What did the brothers think about it?"

"This is what I'm going to tell you tomorrow, if Allah wills. I'm going to bed."'

13

*After our company gathered round the stove the next
evening, Mother said, 'Grandfather had hardly sat down
in his usual place than he looked at each one of us
searchingly, and said . . .'*

I suppose, my children, you are desperately keen to
know what my brothers thought when they knew
I had bought a house without consulting them. In
actual fact, I had made as big a blunder as it was
possible for me to make, but I had been led on by
circumstances. And if I was convinced that when
they saw this house my brothers would be
delighted at what I had done, I wouldn't have

bought it however good the bargain.

It was my practice to go to the shop each day half an hour at least before my brothers. It was my job to open up the shop for the cleaning man who would already be waiting. He would then clean and tidy up the shop before my brothers arrived.

But that morning I arrived three hours after my usual time. Abu Qasim and I had walked down from Salihiya to Marja Square. The Lands Department was in one of the roads branching off the square. We had to wait an hour for Khawaja Yusuf who was staying with a relation in the Christian quarter. We registered the deeds and the exchange of ownership. This also took quite a time. When I finally reached the shop there were, fortunately, no customers around. 'Abd al-Samad looked at me angrily and sternly,

'And where have you been?' he shouted. 'What has been going on? You stayed with friends away from the house and here you are, three hours late. Did you give your brothers any thought? Did it not occur to you that we might get worried about you? Is one whole day not enough for your rest and recreation?

'By Allah, I was not resting or amusing myself; I am late because I've had important business to see to.'

'And what, in the name of Allah, might this important business be?'

'I bought a house yesterday in Salihiya, and this

morning I've been to register it at the Lands Department.'

As I spoke he stared at me, dumbfounded. He then called to Ahmad, my other brother, 'Come here, Ahmad. Come and listen to this. In the name of Allah, your brother has started buying houses and registering them in his name, without asking us about it and seeking our advice. As if we have no connection with him at all!' Ahmad ran in from the front of the shop and stood before me.

'Is what 'Abd al-Samad says true or is he joking?' said Ahmad, in tones no less severe. 'Do you have enough money to buy houses?'

'I know that all he has is twenty-five golden sovereigns,' said 'Abd al-Samad, 'which he has put aside penny by penny so – according to what he has told me – he can travel to Daghestan and see his mother. That's not enough to buy houses, however small or modest they may be.'

'I borrowed the balance.'

As soon as I said this 'Abd al-Samad exploded.

'Has any member of our family ever stretched out his hand to somebody else to borrow money? Have you forgotten Father's advice which he was always repeating: Guard against getting into debt. It is a shame by day, and a worry by night.'

'Let me explain – '

Before I could complete my sentence he had raised his hand and slapped me hard on the cheek. I will never forget it. It has been the only time in my life that I have been struck.

'Get out of my sight,' he said. 'I don't want ever to see your face again.'

Ahmad added, 'Some swindler has doubtless had a good laugh at his expense — tricked him and fleeced him of all his money.'

I left the shop feeling lost and not knowing what to do. I then decided to go home and change and then go back to Abu Qasim al-Salihani and tell him what had happened. Perhaps he could get me out of the mess he had got me into.

I unlocked the door to our house and went in. 'Abd al-Samad's wife was in the courtyard watering the flowerbeds around the fountain. She looked at me.

'May Allah keep evil away from us, Salih, my son. What's the matter with you? Why are you back so early? Are you ill? You don't look at all well.'

'I've come to collect my belongings. 'Abd al-Samad has thrown me out of the house.'

'It is not possible that 'Abd al-Samad would do this. He loves you as he loves his own children. You must have done something to have made him turn against you so suddenly.'

'I will admit to you that I have made a mistake, but he won't listen to me. He actually slapped me on the cheek and told me to get out and that he didn't want to see my face again. If he had listened to me he would have been persuaded of my point of view and have excused me.'

'If he told you not to show your face to him again, that doesn't necessarily mean he's thrown you out of the house. That was a moment of anger when the Devil was at work. Tell me, what did you do? Maybe I can do something to prevent the situation getting out of hand.'

'Do you really want to help me?'

'Do you have to ask? I will do everything I can to help you.'

I threw myself into her arms and kissed her hands warmly. She started to weep. 'That's enough, Salih, that's enough, my son. Tell me, what do you want me to do?'

'I want you to put your headscarf on and come with me. I will explain everything on the way. If you do not do what I ask you now I'll take my clothes and leave the house, never to return. Allah's lands are far-flung.'

'Heaven forbid that I let you take your things and leave this house. I will do whatever you would like me to do, even if it upsets your brother.'

She straightaway put on her headscarf and came out with me. We took a horse-cab to Salihiya and on the way I told her the story of my purchase of the house in every detail. She did not seem convinced.

'If you had wanted to buy a house, my son, there are heaps of houses up for sale in Damascus. Why do you have to go to Salihiya, so far away? There is no doubt in my mind that your brothers would have helped you more than Abu Qasim al-Salihani who is not connected to us. I am afraid he may have been playing some trick on you.'

'Dear sister, don't accuse the poor fellow. By Allah, he is an honest man who wanted only my welfare. I was not thinking of buying any house. Otherwise I would have consulted my brothers, but this house turned up quite suddenly. It was an opportunity I could not let slip. I bought it, as I told you, at a third of its market price.'

'You are so good-natured that you'll believe what anyone tells you. Is it reasonable for anyone to sell his house at one third of the market price?'

'I'll not argue the case with you. You must make up your mind when you see the house.'

'I'd like to do just that.'

We remained silent until we reached the house. When she went into the courtyard she stopped in amazement just as I had done when I saw the house for the first time. She looked around to the right and to the left. Her inspection went from the courtyard to the water-wheel, to the river and to the flowers.

'Never have I seen such a lovely house,' she said. 'I can hardly believe you bought it for only forty golden sovereigns.' When I took her to the outer house she said, 'I confess. You are completely in the right. It was a rare opportunity to buy this house, even though you had to borrow a small sum. May Allah forgive me for having talked ill of your friend, Abu Qasim. He is beyond reproach.'

'I'll stay here until my brothers are persuaded,' I told her. 'The horse-cab is still waiting for us. You can take it back yourself. Try to get my brothers to come and see me when they go riding on Friday. They may change their minds just as you have.'

'I seek refuge in Allah. I will not let you be at loggerheads for a whole week. You stay here and I'll take the cab to the shop. I'll insist on your brothers closing up the shop and coming with me here. The problem will then be solved peacefully, if Allah wills. In our family there has never been a row that has led to a break in relations.'

'I don't know how to thank you, dear sister. I'll never forget this kindness as long as I live,'

'You know how much I think of you. There's no need for words.'

She then got up. I went with her to the cab, said goodbye and wished her all success. I entrusted her to the driver and told him where the shop was.

'If by the call to sunset prayer you have not returned I'll know that you have failed in your efforts,' I told her.

'Hush, man, I've never failed at all in all my life,' she said as she waved me goodbye.

I was already an admirer of this sister-in-law of mine. She ran the household perfectly and never disregarded anybody's interests. But I had never realized she had such self-confidence; clearly she did not doubt her ability to get my brothers to close up the shop and follow her wherever she chose. Ahmad's wife was quite the opposite. She had a weak personality and was incapable of imposing her will on anything, even her own children. There is no doubt that the difference between the two women meant that the house ran smoothly and peacefully. We never had those rows that usually take place in other families that live all under the same roof.

As soon as the horse-cab was out of sight I went back into the house. I rolled up my sleeves, took off my shoes and washed down the courtyard. I watered the flowerbeds, sprinkling them so that they would look their most beautiful. I then brought out chairs and placed them round the fountain. I went into the kitchen to see whether I would be able to make some coffee. I found that that good man, Khawaja Yusuf – may Allah honour and keep him – had left some behind, as well as a coffee-pot and some porcelain cups. I lit some coke in the stove and put the coffee-pot on it. I had only just finished doing this when I heard a knock at the door. My heart was pounding with happiness for I was absolutely sure that my sister-in-law had succeeded in her aim. I opened the door and there she was.

She said, 'Kiss your brothers' hands. They have come to give you their blessing. I did what you told me to do.'

At this 'Abd al-Samad embraced me, kissed me

and said, 'How could you be so bold as to tell your sister-in-law that I had thrown you out of the house? I told you to go and not to show your face. I only meant that for the moment. I was afraid of unleashing upon you the full amount of my anger.'

'May Allah overlook what has passed,' his wife said. 'Come in and have a look at this matchless gem.'

We went into the courtyard. 'Abd al-Samad looked round and then said to his wife, 'By Allah, you were not exaggerating at all, Umm Muhammad. It really is a superb house. Salih, let me have a look at the contract so I can be completely at ease.'

I handed the contract over to him and we sat down round the fountain. He studied it carefully while I got up and went to the kitchen to prepare some coffee. I poured it into the cups and brought it out.

'It's a sound contract, without any flaws,' 'Abd al-Samad said. 'I can now say to you: May Allah bless you, brother Hajj Salih.'

'Your parents would be proud of you,' added his wife.

'Do you think my mother would be satisfied with me?'

'Of course, my son. If she was not satisfied Allah would not have given you such success.'

'This house! by Allah!' said my brother Ahmad, 'could be a beautiful rest-house. What do you say to our closing the shop and opening a coffee-house here? I'm sure most Damascenes would come out here. We'd make more profits than we do from the shop.'

We all laughed and 'Abd al-Samad said, 'That would give amusement to the people of Damascus for ages. They would say, "What times are these? The sons of Mufti al-Hajj Muhammad Jabali al-Daghestani have become coffee-sellers?"'

We all laughed again.

When my brothers saw the outhouse they were even more delighted.

'The poor man, who owned this house – to have sold it for only forty gold sovereigns,' observed Ahmad. 'I pity him.'

'What else could he do?' I said. 'The house had been up for sale for a whole month. He was waiting for a purchaser, but Allah sent him none. He had to travel, because half his family – his sons – were already in America. The other half – his wife and daughters – were in Beirut waiting for him to arrive before the boat set sail. By Allah, if I had had more money I would have paid him, but he seemed to me to be completely satisfied. He gave me his blessing from the bottom of his heart, and my conscience was at ease. But I have omitted to show you some of the furniture we bought from him. Come and look.'

I then took them to one of the small rooms and showed them the bedsteads, chairs and trunks that were stored there.

'These things are all superb,' said my sister-in-law. 'They alone are enough to furnish this huge house. Tomorrow I'll go shopping and select some material that will be suitable for the furniture. I'll also get some curtains. I'll take Salih with me. He'll be sure to find an upholsterer in Salihiya. I want one to do the mattresses and another to do the curtains. In one week's time, if Allah wills, you will find your house, Salih, furnished in the best possible manner.'

'May Allah keep you for me, sister.'

'You must realize,' she went on, 'that the whole family will come here every Friday and spend the day here. And when the schools are closed we'll spend all the summer here in this house of yours.'

'I beg you, sister, don't say "your house" say "our house". It belongs to all of us.'

'May Allah bless you, Hajj Salih,' said 'Abd al-Samad. 'Don't you realize that we must get back to the shop. The cab is still waiting for us.'

At that we all got up and piled into the cab that took us down the road to Damascus. I felt totally happy and satisfied.

Mother said, 'Grandfather then got up and said, "Tomorrow I'll give you a surprise with events that will not have occurred to you at all."'

14

Mother said, 'When we were gathered the next night, I recall Grandfather talked a lot about 'Abd al-Samad's wife. He used to call her his big sister and addressed her as Umm Muhammad. He said...'

My sister, Umm Muhammad, was quite unique. She was remarkable in every respect. As soon as she was persuaded about some idea she would set out to do it all herself.

Early the following week we were having breakfast and she said, 'You will find me at the shop shortly. I want to select some of the material that we're going to need to furnish the Salihiya house.'

'Why are you in so much of a hurry?' asked 'Abd al-Samad.

'Why put off to tomorrow what we can do today? Rest assured, I'll charge you only for the cost of the upholstering, and that will be quite modest. Perhaps all we need is some wool and some cotton.'

'Do you imagine, Umm Muhammad,' said my brother Ahmad, 'that the cloth you take from the shop came to us as a charitable offering in the name of Allah? Did we not have to pay for it?'

'It belongs to all of us,' she said with a laugh. 'We will not be paying for it, but Allah will reward you with good things.'

'Blankets and quilts and mattresses, and kitchen utensils, where are they all coming from?' asked 'Abd al-Samad.

'Don't worry. We've got plenty of those. Do you not remember when we furnished this house we set up one room for guests where we put plenty of mattresses, pillows and quilts? We have not had a single guest who has slept in them. They used to be all piled in the cubby-hole. When Salih moved there they were in the way and I divided them up in different rooms about the house. I thought at one stage I might sell them. Thanks be to Allah, I didn't. We now need them.'

A little later when we were at the shop my sister came and began to pick out curtains and covers for mattresses and stuffing for pillows.

'That's enough, Umm Muhammad,' said 'Abd

al-Samad eventually. 'This way we'll empty the stock in the shop.'

'Offer a prayer to he Prophet,' she laughed. 'These things have become old and you're not depriving customers of anything. Allah will reward you with better things. Come, Salih, my lad, let's carry all this to the house. We'll then go on to the Salihiya house. Salih won't be back at the shop before midday.'

'As you please, Umm Muhammad,' said Ahmad.

My other brother turned aside without saying a word. His wife had him under control.

I carried all the things my sister had selected. We took them first to the family house and before long there was piled up in the courtyard all manner of furnishings, kitchenware and lamps.

'How shall we get all this to Salihiya?' she asked. 'The only way is to hire a cart to take all that. We can go in a cab.'

'Go ahead then.'

Soon a cart and a horse-cab were outside the house. We packed most of the things on to the cart, and the rest, especially the more fragile items such as the lamps, on to the cab.

When we arrived at the Salihiya house we offloaded everything. I then set off in search of upholsterers. I soon found a couple, one for the curtains, the other for the furnishings. Umm Muhammad told them to do things exactly as she instructed. She insisted that the work be completed by Friday morning, that is, in four days' time. They agreed, for she was generous with a tip.

Next Friday we went riding, I and my brothers and their sons, Muhammad and Mustafa, who were just beginning to learn how to ride. We went on to the house.

I could hardly believe my eyes. My sisters-in-law and their four daughters had cleaned the house, arranged the furniture and hung the curtains. They had placed a table in the courtyard so we could enjoy looking at the garden, the stream, the water-wheel and the fountain as we ate.

'Before we eat,' said Umm Muhammad, 'come and let me show you this room now that it has been furnished. It's really lovely.'

The room that was to the right of the *liwan* was as spacious as a reception room. At the top end were windows that overlooked the garden. To the left were windows that looked on to the courtyard. She had arranged some chairs there which had been upholstered and provided with cushions. All had been covered in brightly coloured Damascene fabrics. Curtains which went with the furnishings had been hung up. A Persian carpet had been laid on the floor with matching colouring. I have no idea where Umm Muhammad had got that from. In the corners at the end of the room she had placed the two black walnut wood chests that were inlaid with bright mother of pearl. An elegant lamp was on each chest.

'This is the best and largest room,' she said. 'It cannot be taken over by one person so I have turned it into a reception room for us all. We shall also be able to receive guests here. As for the other rooms, I've put the beds and other furnishings there so they can be ready whenever we need them, if we spend the summer here.'

My nephew Muhammad – he was a bright lad, easy-going and with a sense of humour – then said to his mother, 'Is there no cubby-hole here for Uncle Salih?'

'Hush, my boy. May Allah cut off your impudent tongue. You're very cheeky. I've prepared a room for your uncle that would suit a princely bridegroom.'

We sat down around the table and tucked into the rice and beans, the green beans with spring onion, the tarragon and yoghurt. We ate with a relish that made us forget everything but the food. None of us spoke a word as we were very hungry after the riding. When we had finished we sat round the fountain and drank coffee.

'Salih, my son, may Allah reward you for your purchase of this house,' said Umm Muhammad. 'It has provided a wonderful amenity to our way of life. We women and children, especially the girls, we've spent more than ten years in the city of Damascus and not once have we seen this lovely area at the foot of Jabal Qasyun. We do at least have memories of our land of Daghestan. As for you men, you're accustomed to coming here every Friday to ride and then picnic in these charming spots while we women wait for you to return to the house that was always gloomy and dark.'

'In the name of Allah Almighty,' said her husband, 'women are never satisfied. Now you are seeing the house as gloomy and dark when you used to see it as a lovely place: indeed you used to boast about it.'

'Now that I look at it in comparison with this house, I see it very differently, and I swear that you will too. Like all men, you like to boast about appearances.'

'All I have ever asked of my Lord is that He assign me to you. Who can get the better of you in any argument, woman?'

We all laughed at this tiff between 'Abd al-Samad and his wife. Then Umm Mustafa, Ahmad's wife, said, 'Do you know what's missing from this house?'

'What's that?' I asked.

'It needs a bride.'

'Who do you want a bride for?'

'I want one for you, of course. Do you imagine I am suggesting a bride for one of your brothers so we might have a co-wife in our old age?'

'I seek Allah's mercy. I will not think of getting married until I have paid off my debts completely. I will then save money enough to go back to Daghestan and see mother. For the moment I'm not giving marriage a thought. I raised a loan on one occasion in order to purchase this house. My reward was a slap on the left of my face the sting of which I shall never forget. Should I borrow some more money in order to get married and earn another slap on the right of my face? No, no, a thousand times no, my lady. May Allah make me free from need.'

'Haven't you forgotten, Hajj Salih, that slap arose from a misunderstanding,' said 'Abd al–Samad. 'Did we not wipe it away with a kiss?'

'Yes, we did wipe it away. I'll not mention the subject again.'

'Getting Salih married would be very difficult,' said Umm Muhammad.

'Why should it be so difficult?' asked Ahmad. 'Solutions follow problems.'

'I once said to Salih that when he grew up it would be time for him to get married. He told me that if I found a girl like his mother then he would marry her at once.'

'Unless you change your mind, Salih,' said Ahmad, 'you've got a long wait. Your mother was a rare beauty.'

'I will make an excuse out of the virtue of patience.'

'Don't worry,' said Umm Muhammad. 'From this day on I'm going to start looking for a girl that is like your mother. I'm sure I'll find one, if Allah wills.'

'May Allah preserve you for ever, dear sister,' I said.

I felt immensely happy as I gazed at all my family, especially at my nephews as they played in the garden and on the banks of the stream. But there was also a lump in my throat. I had paid a very high price. I had intended at the beginning of this summer to be in Daghestan, in Mother's arms. Realizing this ambition was now postponed for many years, I had first to pay off my debts and then to start saving again. I did not know how much time this would take. I was woken up from these reveries by 'Abd al-Samad's voice.

'The sun's beginning to go down. We must get ready to go back. How can we get a horse-cab to take the women?'

'Not to worry,' I said. 'I've already taken care of the problem. I arranged with the driver of the cab that brought them here to come just before sunset. I made sure he'd come by not paying his fare.'

'You've learned to think of everything, brother. But don't worry about the fare. I'll settle it.'

Mother said, 'Grandfather rose with the words, "That's enough for today. We'll come back to it tomorrow night, if Allah wills."'

15

Mother said, 'Grandfather resumed his tale...'

Two years went by. I scrimped and saved penny upon penny until I was able to pay back Abu Qasim al-Salihani. But I have omitted to tell you that I bought a horse before I redeemed the debt. That too was thanks to the influence of my adopted uncle, Abu Qasim. He was most persuasive in winning people over. One day I invited him and his sons to dinner at the Salihiya house. It had been purchased with his help and I wanted him to see the house fully furnished. Abu Qasim and his sons were impressed with the arrangements.

'You once complained to me,' he said, 'that after your father died you had to sleep in some tiny room at your Bab al-Barid house. This upset you.'

'I still sleep there to this day.'

'My son, how can you have such a spacious house and still choose to sleep in some cramped cubby-hole?'

'What can I do? If I chose to sleep here every night, it would be both expensive and exhausting. I'd have to hire a cab each evening, and walk down to the shop every morning. It's quite a distance.'

'Has it not occurred to you to buy a horse? You like riding.'

'I would love to own a horse, but I don't have the ready cash to buy one.'

'Listen to me. A first-rate young horse costs no more than three golden sovereigns. I've got such a horse and could sell it to you today if you so wished.'

Abu Qasim bred horses on his farm for the market.

'Is it permissible to incur an additional debt before I have paid off the earlier one?'

'Just imagine that the debt was for twenty sovereigns, not seventeen. Have I not told you many times that I am surer of my money when it is being used by you than if it were in a trunk, liable to be stolen at any time?'

'Thank you, Uncle Abu Qasim, for your confidence in me. May Allah never take you away from us. But I can make no commitment until I have consulted my brothers. I don't want to go through what I went through when I bought the house.'

'I won't sell the horse until I've heard from you.'

Next day I put the matter to my brothers, saying that I wanted to sleep at the Salihiya house. 'Abd al-Samad said testily, 'So you want to get deeper into debt.'

I told him what Abu Qasim had said. He reflected on the subject and then said, 'Once one has got into debt, what is the difference between a loan of seventeen golden sovereigns and a loan of twenty from the same source? There is no doubt that Abu Qasim is well intentioned towards you. By Allah, if I had the ready money to pay for such a horse, I would buy it for you, but you know that I have committed all spare cash to goods for the forthcoming season. All I have left is enough for the running costs of the household. But don't buy the horse before I see it and cast my eye over it.'

'Abd al-Samad had some experience of horses gained from the horsemen of Daghestan.

'You can have a look at the horse on Friday after we've been riding.'

'Don't forget that a horse needs a stable.'

'There's a small building at the end of the outer garden. It may have been for a servant or for a gardener. It could be converted into a stable.'

'There's no longer any problem then.'

My brother Ahmad then said, 'I think somebody

ought to stay overnight at the Salihiya house, particularly as it has now been furnished. The contents should be kept secure from burglars.'

'I am given to understand that the area is said to be secure,' I said. 'But it's better to be safe than sorry.'

'This means, Salih,' said Ahmad, 'that you'll be leaving your home before you need to – that is, before you get married.'

'Good heavens, no, I will not be leaving you, except when it is time for bed. I'll come each morning and have breakfast with you as usual. We'll come back from the shop to the house for dinner in the evening and after that I'll get on my horse and go up to Salihiya for the night.'

'That's good, because if you left us, it would be hard on us all.'

Next Friday after we had been riding we went to Abu Qasim's paddock. My brothers became acquainted with him and his sons. 'Abd al-Samad thanked him for his interest in me. Abu Qasim then brought out the horse. It was really a fine animal, handsomely black with a white mane and a long tail. 'Abd al-Samad inspected it thoroughly and was happy with it, giving his consent to my purchase of it. He then invited Abu Qasim and his sons to lunch. I felt pleased with the gracious gesture on 'Abd al-Samad's part towards my friends. But I asked him on the way to the house, 'What, I wonder, are we going to give our guests to eat?'

153

'Umm Muhammad has ordered *safiha* and cheese pastries from the best baker in Bab al–Barid.'

Umm Muhammad soon afterwards turned up at the house with the rest of the family. They brought the *safiha*, the cheese pastries and also clotted cream pancakes as well.

My nieces started to lay the table in the *liwan*, while we men sat in the garden, enjoying the gentle breeze and the leafy shade.

After lunch we moved to the large reception room for coffee. As we sipped our coffee we talked about the revolt in Daghestan. Abu Qasim had heard the imam of the mosque after Friday prayers calling on the worshippers to pray for victory for Shaikh Shamil, the leader of the revolt who was battling against the Russian Empire. Thanks to his courage and the strength of his convictions he had been victorious, in spite of the great difference in numbers and weaponry between the two sides. 'Abd al–Samad told Abu Qasim proudly a lot about the Daghestani revolt and about Shaikh Shamil, the great youthful leader renowned for his courage and his dash, his single-mindedness, his piety and his sense of justice. All Daghestan was at his feet. He had managed to unite many different tribes under one banner and as a result was a thorn in Russia's flesh. Abu Qasim was amazed as he listened to my brother talking of the masterly horsemanship of his fellow Daghestanis as they battled in the mountains, forcing the Russian armies on to the defensive.

I listened to the conversation without participating. I felt rather distressed for I accepted Father's view which he had confided to me when we were in Mecca after I had asked him about the revolt.

I recalled his words, 'This revolt, my boy, is bound to fail. There are no two ways about it. Daghestan is not able to vanquish the Russian Empire so long as it fails to get the backing of any other state in that part of the world, such as the Ottoman Empire. And the Ottoman Empire has washed its hands of the revolt. In such circumstances we have to keep calm and to control our innermost feelings. We should not be misled by short-term victories. We must do our best to reach an understanding with Russia and negotiate conditions that guarantee our freedom to worship and our self-rule.'

I remember Father repeating with great feelings of distress, 'What a loss, oh my country, my Daghestan. How I mourn for your horsemen so bold who have died in vain.'

Several years had gone by since then and the revolt went on and on. I was filled with despair in my soul about ever meeting Mother again. Especially so when I learnt that the borders of Daghestan had been virtually sealed off, for the Russians had imposed a blockade to cut off any supplies coming in from abroad.

I was now fairly well off, but what was the point of thinking of going there if I was unable to travel because of the war and the closure of the frontiers? Members of the family asked me from time to time why I was so preoccupied. I seldom laughed or chatted. They seemed unaware of the reasons for my troubled state of mind. I frequently reproached myself with having bought the house rather than going to Daghestan before the revolt had reached such an intensity and conditions had become so difficult. I constantly wondered what news there was of Mother. Was she ageing? How many children did she have? Was she living comfortably or was she encountering hardships? Did she think of me as I thought of her? She must have thought of me and blamed me for failing in my duty towards her. It had been possible for me to go to her but not for her to come to me.

When summer arrived the family moved to the Salihiya house. But the family was smaller now and not so bubbling with gaiety as it had been, for my four nieces had all been married in the previous winter months one after the other.

With astonishment we interrupted Grandfather, "How did that happen, Grandfather, so suddenly?"
He said, "I will explain."

When the revolt in Daghestan intensified and affected the whole region we were sure that it was going to be acutely difficult for the family to go back. It would be a venture fraught with unbearable consequences. Men on horseback might be able to traverse the long distance and scale those mountains, but not women and children.

One day while the girls were in the kitchen washing up after dinner, my sister-in-law Umm Muhammad took advantage of their absence and said, 'I am very concerned at present about the prospects of our girls getting married before they get too old. Our oldest is over eighteen and it is becoming hard to find good husbands. If they were not so attractive and well brought up and did not enjoy so good a reputation I would despair of them ever getting married. What concerns me is that no young man from Damascus has come forward to make an offer. The word has got around that Daghestani girls do not marry Damascenes because people think we expect to return to our fatherland and we would be reluctant to leave our daughters behind far from us, strangers in this land.

'But,' she added, 'I think I know how to handle the matter and I pray for the blessing of Allah.' We did not ask how she proposed to handle the matter. This was one of those guarded secrets of hers that she chose not to divulge until she had achieved her objective.

One month later suitors started calling on us. We made a selection of those whom we thought measured up to our girls. Eventually within a few months all four were married off to young men from the best Damascus families.

Wedding celebrations were held to which the cream of the ladies of Damascus were invited.

From that time on we felt that we had become integrated into the Damascus community more than before. Our new in-laws invited us to parties at their houses and we in turn invited them to feasts at our houses. Umm Muhammad always preferred to hold parties in the spring at the Salihiya house because it was grander than our Bab al-Barid house. All our guests were astonished and full of admiration for our other establishment. In this way ties of friendship were forged between ourselves and many of the leading people of Damascus who were now connected to us by marriage.

One evening we urged Umm Muhammad to explain how she was able to find husbands for the girls in such a short time. Had she, we wondered, resorted to magic? What did she do?

'In Allah's name,' she said, 'I resorted to no magic – I don't believe in it. All I did was whisper a few words into the ear of the woman in charge of the *hammam*. She it was who obtained such rapid results.'

'What were these few words that were so magically effective?' we asked.

'She is very fond of me. She holds me in favour because I have been generous to her with tips. On one occasion after I had had a bath and came to pay the fee I paid her double; I leant over and whispered, "If anybody wishes to make an offer to one of our girls, tell him to come to the house. We've decided not to go back to Daghestan, but to stay here in Damascus. We would like to marry our girls to Damascenes."

"'I wish you had told me this ages ago," she said, "because many of our respectable customers have asked me the way to your house after they have seen your girls here. But I have always told them not to bother because Daghestani families only marry their daughters off to Daghestanis. I said you'd be going back to your country and would marry the girls there. But now I know what to do."

'I promised her that each time one of our girls got married I would give her a valuable present which she would like. She said I was kindness itself. I told her only to send us young men who were worthy of our girls. She nodded, saying, "I will surprise you, Umm Muhammad. You don't need to tell me."

'This crabby old woman managed to do all I asked most competently, as you now know.'

'What a pity, dear sister,' said my brother Ahmad, 'that you were created a woman. By Allah, if you had been born a man you would have been like Shaikh Shamil.'

We all laughed. Then 'Abd al-Samad said, 'Spare us, Ahmad, don't give her ideas above her station.'

'Have no fear, Abu Muhammad,' said his wife. 'I

know my limits and will keep within them.'

Mother said, 'Grandfather stopped his narrative, got up and said, "Good night, my children. Sweet dreams. We'll meet again tomorrow, if Allah wills."'

16

Mother said, 'I remember Grandfather starting the next evening with the words...'

What concerned us most those days was news of the revolt in Daghestan. Our leader, Shaikh Shamil, had acquired a huge reputation throughout all the lands of Islam. People in one country would pass on to people in another country news of the revolt, and tales of the heroic deeds performed by his Daghestani followers, and of all those who helped him with impatient zeal. Some reports beggared belief and there was of course some exaggeration.

With the coming of summer the family moved,

as had become our habit, to the Salihiya house.

It was the custom in Damascus for married daughters to call on their families once a month, bringing their children and staying for three days. The husband would come on the last day and see his in-laws and take his wife and children back to their own home. When he arrived there would be quite a feast. Sometimes the son-in-law would be accompanied by his mother or his sisters. Umm Muhammad used to set aside the first three days of each week for the visit of one of her daughters. In this way there would be a feast once a week. 'Abd al-Samad used to grumble about the expense.

'Allah provides,' his wife answered him, 'and you don't know where His provision comes from. I believe in the adage, "Spend what you have in hand and all will be cared for." Or do you want us to treat our daughters not as well as our Damascene friends do? No, a thousand times no. This will never happen so long as I have anything to do with it...'

Against his better judgement my brother held his tongue.

It was very hot that summer. One day I came back early from the shop just before sunset prayers. Umm Muhammad received me with a cheerful smile on her face. 'I've found her, Salih,' she said.

'Found whom?'

'The bride who takes after your mother.'

'Can this be true?'

'Ask your sister, Umm Mustafa.'

'By Allah, Salih,' said Umm Mustafa, 'as soon as I saw her we exchanged glances, your sister and I. We then both said she was like Umm Salih when your parents got married. She was, I suppose, about the same age as this young lady is today.'

'For the last three years,' Umm Muhammad said, 'I've been searching for a girl who looks even slightly like your mother but I never succeeded. But this girl really is so like her: jet-black hair, soft pure white skin, a lovely round face, sparkling wide-open dark eyes, but – to be quite frank, she is not as tall as your mother.'

'Is she very short?' I asked.

'She's not short, but she is not tall and thin, nor is she slender-necked like your mother.'

'Where did you see this young lady?'

'Umm Mustafa and I went today to the 'Afif *hammam* near here in Salihiya. As we were undressing this young girl came in with a middle-aged woman. They sat down on the platform near where we were sitting. I felt from their features that they were not from Damascus. I went up to them and greeted them. I told them that we were Daghestanis and they at once said, "From the land of Shaikh Shamil? May Allah grant him victory."

'I told them who we were and asked them where they were from. The young lady told me they were from Georgia not far from Daghestan. They arrived in Damascus three three years ago.

163

The girl's Arabic was as fluent as ours and we've been here for fifteen years. She seems to be bright. The older lady was her aunt and I talked to her and learnt that the girl's parents were both dead and that she had been adopted by her aunt who had no children of her own. There had been a civil war in Georgia between Christians and Muslims that had been exacerbated by the Russians. The girl's father had fallen a victim, and her mother had no option but to sell off her property and furniture and join some refugees who had decided to migrate to Damascus.'

'You've excited my interest in this girl,' I said. 'When will you be able to arrange an engagement?'

'Tomorrow if you wish. I asked the aunt about their house and she showed me where it was as if she could read what was in my mind. It's in the Muhajirin quarter, not so very far from where we are at present.'

One month after this conversation your grandfather became a bridegroom. The family arranged a magnificent wedding ceremony at the Salihiya house like all other Damascene weddings. We invited many of the neighbours and people we knew from Bab al-Barid, as well as people from Salihiya. We also invited all our Damascene in-laws. Abu Qasim insisted on dressing me up for the wedding at his house. I went in procession from his house to ours. I was surrounded by young men who chanted the songs that are traditionally chanted for the bridegroom. I went into the house with my brothers and we were greeted by ululations from the womenfolk. I felt a bit embarrassed when I finally found myself in the bride's presence. I was almost in tears. But with a big effort I managed to pull myself together. It is very difficult when your mood swings from one extreme to another: elation and grief. You never know on which to concentrate.

I felt an enormous sense of elation when I looked up at the bride and saw that she really was like Mother. I fell in love with this girl who became my companion for the rest of my life.

I also felt an intense grief tugging at my heart because Mother was deprived of this joyful occasion to which mothers look forward from the day they give birth to their sons. I insisted on my bride's aunt coming to live with us to keep my bride company. She agreed. I was delighted about this for I didn't have to worry about my wife whenever I was away from the house.

There were no changes in our way of life after I got married. Our family still used to spend Fridays in winter at the Salihiya house, and would all move in for the whole of the summer months. I would often host dinners for the in-laws of my nieces in order to take some of the load off my brothers' shoulders. My wife and her aunt got on well with all my family. One year after the marriage I was blessed with a son whom I called Najib. That is your father, and may Allah preserve him for you, my children. Allah did not bless me with any other child, so I was very attached to Najib and looked forward to the hour of returning to the house from the moment I left it.

One day about two years after my marriage a huge man in Kurdish dress called at our shop. He greeted us and asked, 'Which of you is Salih al-Daghestani?'

I went up to him. 'I am Salih al-Daghestani,' I said.

'His Honour the Governor of the Pilgrimage, Sa'id Pasha al-Yusuf, wishes to see you now.'

My brothers and I looked at each other. What was it all about? Then 'Abd al-Samad whispered in my ear, 'I recall that Father was a very good friend of the Pasha. It may be that the Pasha wishes to entrust you with some job, so behave in the right way.'

I went with this huge man to Souk Saruja where the Pasha lived. We went into a house that was opulent in its size and style.

'Wait here a moment while I announce your arrival to the Pasha,' said my escort. A little later he came back and led me to a vast hall in the middle of which sat the Pasha on a fine chair. He was a man of great dignity. I felt he was inspecting me with a penetrating gaze as I entered the room. I was embarrassed. When I went up to him I gave a bow and kissed his hand.

'You are Salih, son of the mufti, al-Hajj Muhammad al-Jabali?' he asked.

'Yes, sir.'

'May Allah have mercy on your father. He was a very good friend of mine. I once heard from him that he had a son called Salih who had obtained a certificate in accounts and bookkeeping at a very young age. This showed he had great talent in this field.'

'That is me, sir. I still practise the profession in our shop.'

'I wish to bestow upon you the post of treasurer of the Pilgrimage. I know your father was a man of courage, a man of religion, a man of nobility. And the son must take after the father in skills and intuition.'

'I'm at your service. May Allah prolong your life, my honourable Pasha.'

'You will carry out your duties, my son, during the months of the Pilgrimage, that is, for only four months in the year. I will allocate a satisfactory salary for you. You will travel with us at the start of the Pilgrimage season, that is, in one month's time. The retiring treasurer will travel with you this year. He has become an old man and is exhausted by all the travelling. But he will show you how to do the job.'

'If Allah wills, I will do my best to win your satisfaction, sir.'

I went away from him feeling delighted but at

the same time apprehensive for I would be away from my wife, child and home for four months out of every twelve. Even when I was in Damascus I could not wait for the day to be over so that I could get back to them and share my life with them.

I returned to my brothers and talked with them about what the Pasha had said. They congratulated me on the lofty rank I had attained and wished me every success.

As for my wife, it was not good news for her that I would be away from her for a third of each year. She tried to dissuade me from taking the post however beneficial it might be. I explained to her that it was not for me to refuse such a boon that had fallen from the sky into my lap. It may in fact make our life more comfortable and our future more assured, especially as we were in the prime of life as far as energy and opportunity were concerned. She began to cry and pleaded with me to take her with me. This prompted that good woman, her aunt, to reason with her until she calmed down and accepted the inevitable, but with no great enthusiasm.

The next month went by with extraordinary speed. I packed my bags and made my way to the Pasha's house at the prescribed time. From there we got into some horse-cabs, I and some of the officials who were accompanying the Pasha. We reached al-'Asali where the pilgrims waited until the usual customs had been completed. Cannons fired, announcing the start of the Pilgrimage caravan. One of the Pasha's staff introduced me to the retiring treasurer whose place I was taking. He was an elderly man, distinguished and mild-tempered. I felt a bit awkward when I met him because I seemed to be displacing him. What could I do but bend over his hand and kiss it? He gently touched my shoulder.

'May Allah bless you, my son,' he said. 'May He look after you in this post.' At once any awkwardness in our relationship disappeared. He regarded me as one of his own sons.

A little later a soldier came over and said to us, 'Prepare to mount your horses. We have fastened the treasury on to the camel's back, and the Pilgrimage is about to set off.'

I was taken aback when I realized that I would be travelling in the front just like the Pasha. The old treasurer smiled. 'Did you not know,' he said, 'that this post is one of great prestige. You are the only official who travels in front in a litter like the Pasha's, because the Pilgrimage treasury chest is your responsibility. A group of soldiers will guard the front of the caravan from the moment it leaves Damascus until it arrives in the noble city of Mecca. They will make sure that the treasury chest does not fall into the hands of thieves.'

As soon as we set off the old treasurer explained to me what I had to do, and then handed over to me the book of accounts, the inventories and the keys of the chests. He warned me not to hand out money to anyone, not even the Pasha himself, without obtaining a receipt. I should then keep these receipts in a safe place.

When we got to Mecca he took me round to the houses of the sharifs to give them the fees paid by the sultan in his capacity as Custodian of the Two Holy Places. We began with the Sharif of Mecca, the Governor of Mecca and then the other sharifs. Each large fee made up of golden sovereigns had been put into a small chest of burnished wood with green velvet lining. These chests were sealed and had the name of a particular sharif inscribed on them. We handed over to each sharif his own chest. He broke the seal open, counted the sovereigns and issued us with a receipt. We filed these receipts and forwarded them to the Ottoman government in Constantinople. Smaller fees were handed over in velvet bags.

Can you believe me, children, when I tell you that your grandfather stayed in this post for twenty-five years. Allah awarded me this honour and gave me the pleasure of visiting His time-honoured house repeatedly during these long years.

'Here Grandfather paused again, Mother told us, saying, "I will now bid you goodnight because I am feeling ready for sleep, perhaps more so than you."'

17

Mother said, 'The next evening Grandfather spoke with some sadness...'

The days went by and the years went by, so much like each other that I was unaware of the passage of time.

Four months of my year were spent on the Pilgrimage. I would return to Damascus, full of love and yearning. Each time I would be fearful of bad tidings. Then one year my fears were realized. My brother, 'Abd al-Samad, had gone to his Maker while I was away. I was most distressed, as much as I was when Father died, for my feelings towards

'Abd al-Samad had become those of a son towards his father. What gave me some comfort was that he was quite happy with me, especially after I invited him to go on the Pilgrimage just two years before he passed away. I had asked the Pasha if I might take him with me in the litter. He granted permission.

'How could I withhold permission to the son of my friend, al-Hajj Muhammad al-Jabali?' he said. 'This is the first time I have allowed the treasurer to take one of his relations with him.'

'May Allah never deprive me of your kindness and good feelings, Pasha, sir.'

'Abd al-Samad was very happy during the Pilgrimage. I looked after him personally, making him as comfortable as I could. When he got back to Damascus he would talk about me to his family and friends.

'I have performed the Pilgrimage, and was treated like royalty, thanks to my brother, Salih. May Allah bless him and reward him for being so good. This, my children, this is the way of the world and we have no choice but to accept it.'

The years rolled by, one after the other. We were hardly conscious of the passage of time. I could scarcely believe that my son who seemed only to have just been born was now fifteen. If he had not been about the same height as myself I would not have credited it.

One year I asked the Pasha leave to take some Damascus goods with me and to sell them to traders in Madina and Mecca. My plan was then to purchase some of the articles other pilgrims brought, such as Indian silk and porcelain, and to bring them back to Damascus to sell.

'I grant you permission on the condition that your hand does not touch the money of the treasury which is in your custody. You must not take that money, hoping to make a profit and then return the capital to the treasury. That is absolutely forbidden.'

'Allah forbid that I do any such thing, Pasha, sir. I will buy and sell only with my own money.'

'My confidence in you is great. You never let me down. I know that most officials who trade do so without asking my permission. How then can I withhold permission from you who have asked for it?'

I made incredibly huge profits. I also bought a young slave girl to help my wife with the house-work. Her name was Sabah. I also used to shower presents on each member of the family.

When I was on the Pilgrimage I looked out in my spare time for pilgrims from the Caucasus in order to learn about the revolt in Daghestan. I was especially alert for news about Shaikh Shamil. This man of fabulous stature, mind and faith – how I longed to set eyes on him. His conduct was like that of the ancient prophets. No criticism touched him, and he was stricter with his own family, his sons and his household than with ordinary people.

These pilgrims told me tales of Shaikh Shamil that were quite extraordinary.

Shaikh Shamil and his warriors used to reconnoitre possible battle sites in the mountains. These areas were above the plains through which the Russian armies would march. He liked to ambush the huge army at first light as it crossed the plain. Some Russian soldiers used to scale the rugged mountains that harboured no other warriors but Shaikh Shamil and his detachment.

Sometimes his men suggested that they draw off the soldiers to where there was a larger number of warriors who would be able to take on the Russians. The Russians were bound to pass through the mountains to get to the areas where the Daghestanis had their encampments. But Shaikh Shamil would insist that they themselves, in spite of their small numbers, confront the great army. He said this because he was familiar with all the mountain paths of Daghestan. The Russian army would have no option but to open up and level a road that would take them to an open area in the heart of the mountains, from which other paths would lead to other mountain areas where there were Daghestani bases. Shaikh Shamil would place his small number of men behind the rocks on either side of the road as it climbed up into the mountains. He would order them to act with the utmost self-restraint and not to open fire until the vanguard of the army was almost upon them. When the army was almost upon them – after a long climb into these hills – Shaikh Shamil would fire on them, and his soldiers would follow suit. Within seconds a hail of bullets rained down on the army, spattering them like heavy rain. Before long the Russian army would be thrown into confusion and the road would be littered with the corpses of Russian soldiers. The survivors would turn tail and flee. The number of those who fled was always greater than those who were killed.

With such audacity, intelligence and leadership did Shaikh Shamil outwit his enemies.

'Grandfather told us he heard another tale from those Circassians which I could hardly believe had I not had it confirmed from another source.'

After the war had gone on for a long time some Daghestanis were growing weary of the fighting and came to Shaikh Shamil to try to persuade him to surrender to the Russians. Shaikh Shamil issued a decree that anybody who spoke of surrender would be sentenced to one hundred lashes in public. The party calling for surrender interceded with Shaikh Shamil's mother. They were aware of her standing with her son who would be sure to respond to her if she advocated surrender. When she tried to plead the case, Shaikh Shamil said to his mother, 'Did you not hear the decree about what would happen to those who called for surrender?'

'But I am your mother, Shamil.'

'You are a Daghestani before you are the mother of Shaikh Shamil. So the decree applies to you just as it does to every other Daghestani man or woman.'

He then ordered that his mother be taken to the square. Her face was covered in readiness for a public flogging. People were dumbfounded as they stood watching. Shaikh Shamil was among the spectators.

After she received two or three lashes, Shaikh Shamil addressed the flogger. 'That's enough for now. On my mother's behalf I shall receive the other ninety-seven lashes.'

He gave instructions that his mother be taken home, and he stripped himself preparatory to being flogged.

His staff and his generals tried to dissuade him. 'You are Shaikh Shamil, leader of the whole of Daghestan. Your fame has spread to all corners of the world. Is it possible that you can be flogged in the public square before so many people? It's a scandal for Daghestan.'

But Shaikh Shamil was not a man to go back on his word. The executioner started to flog him, gently.

'Is this how you flog the guilty?' demanded the shaikh. 'Take your shirt off and I'll show you what a flogging should be like.' He proceeded to flog the executioner with all his might. He then handed over the whip, saying 'You must flog me like that, just as you would flog anybody else.'

I don't know whether this story is the actual truth or whether it's one of those legends that are told about heroes. Allah alone knows.

There is one other story I heard.

The Russians captured one of Shaikh Shamil's young sons. The Tsar took him to his palace and brought him up with his own children and became very fond of him. When he was older the Tsar sent him with his own sons to the military academy where he graduated as an officer. Now it happened that Shaikh Shamil had captured three Georgian princesses and the Tsar asked Shaikh Shamil to release them in return for his own son. Shaikh Shamil was content with the proposal and took the princesses to the Daghestan-Russia frontier. But when he saw his own son in Russian military uniform he handed him some Daghestani clothes, saying, 'Take off the uniform of the enemy in the land of the enemy and put on national dress before you step on the land of your own people.'

The young man did what his father told him to do. He then ran up to his father and kissed his hand. They embraced each other with great warmth. Shortly after his return he became aware of the poverty from which the Daghestanis were suffering as a result of the war. He went to his father and recommended submission to Russia on the grounds that Daghestan was small and poor and could never triumph over the mighty Russian Empire however long the war went on. Shaikh Shamil then ordered his son to be imprisoned for defeatism. The son remained in prison until he died of a broken heart three years later.

With such strong faith and exemplary sacrifice did Shaikh Shamil lead the Daghestani revolt for twenty-five whole years. The revolt had broken out a few years before Shaikh Shamil assumed the leadership; it did not involve all parts of the land of Daghestan until Shaikh Shamil took the lead.

I used to have a great feeling of satisfaction, my children, when I heard people expressing their pride in Shaikh Shamil and in the steadfastness and sacrifices of the Daghestani people. At the same time, I used to feel intense agony because I was quite certain that it would end in failure, for as Father used to say, 'Reconciliation with Russia is the safest policy for our country. It is better than war.'

For this reason I have never thought of taking part in the revolt. I shared Father's views and respected his intuition. But it never occurred to me that my country would be able to stand up against the Russian Empire for such a long time. I did not want Father to be wrong in his estimation, though I did wish so at one time.

Was a miracle possible? Could the Russians retreat and sue the Daghestanis for peace? Poor little Daghestan, but proud and precious with its leader and its sons.

But miracles have not taken place on earth for a very long time.

I used to dream by day and by night what I might do if such a miracle were to take place.

Here I was in Damascus living at ease and holding a good position. But I would give it all up with a clear conscience and take my small family to my native town and to my mother's bosom. It would not bother me to live on a pittance in my home town. I would feel spiritually rich, rich in terms of integrity, and of conscience. I would feel pride in my intimate association with my fellow-citizens.

This is true wealth, my children, an inexhaustible wealth, however long you live.

'With the words, "Let us end our tale this evening and let us enjoy sweet dreams," Grandfather paused for the night,' said Mother.

18

Mother said, 'We gathered as usual around Grandfather and this evening every word he uttered was laden with grief.'

When the time of Pilgrimage drew near in the year 1859 I felt the urge to seek the company of pilgrims from the Caucasus, and to talk about the Daghestan revolt and my hero Shaikh Shamil. I never wearied of hearing news of him or of my Daghestani fellow-countrymen. By day and by night I used to dream of victory in Daghestan.

And of the miracle that would amaze the world...

But as I told you, for a long time miracles have not happened in the world.

'He then said very sadly...'

The revolt failed and Shaikh Shamil surrendered.

'We all gasped, our eyes filled with tears,' Mother told us. 'And Grandfather added...'

But Shaikh Shamil was heroic in submission just as he was heroic in his victories.

The first to bear witness to that were his enemies themselves.

The Russians captured him by surprise. He was at his village, Gunib, with just a couple hundred of his supporters. The village was well fortified and surrounded on all four sides by lofty mountains. News reached the Russians that he was there, and they hurried to besiege the village. They climbed up the surrounding mountains with such speed that people said they used ladders. They then stormed the village from all sides.

Shaikh Shamil accepted what happened with outstanding manly fortitude. His soldiers wanted to fight to the death, but he prevented them from doing so. It was difficult for him to sacrifice them in a battle that was bound to fail. What was left for him to do was to put on his uniform, arm himself fully, mount his horse and set off alone to where he was told that the commander of the Russian army, Prince Bariatinsky, was camped in the mountains.

The prince was taken aback when he saw the shaikh standing before him, tall and erect, heavily armed and in full battle dress.

The prince sat down on a rock and gazed at the shaikh for some time. The shaikh remained standing, resting on his sword, head held high, full of dignity and pride, the strong features of his face giving nothing away.

'Your entire struggle, all this fighting, has been to no avail, Shamil,' the prince said. 'Here you are, surrendering.'

'Not at all,' Shaikh Shamil replied calmly and with a steady voice. 'My efforts have not been fruitless, prince. The memory of the struggle will endure for ever in the hearts of our people. My efforts have forged comrades and fighters out of clans that were warring among themselves. We have united scores of villages that were disputing with each other. Out of the many divisions of Daghestan I have moulded one Daghestani nation. I have planted feelings of patriotism, a love of a united Daghestan in the hearts of all Daghestanis. This great national feeling I have created for my grandchildren. Do you consider this a trifling matter?'

To this the prince had nothing to say, not a word.

After a short space of time the prince stipulated

the conditions for the surrender, and Shaikh Shamil was silent, offering no objection. He knew that the defeated have no right to raise objections.

The Russians took their prisoner to the capital, St Petersburg, and he stayed there some time. He was then transferred to the land of Kaluga where he remained a prisoner for eleven years. The Russians treated him well, as befitted such a noble leader. When he asked the Russian government to permit him to go to Mecca in order to perform the Pilgrimage, they granted the request. That was in 1870. Shaikh Shamil made his way to the Holy Places, but he stayed for one year only. In 1871 he answered the summons of his Lord and his pure soul ascended to heaven in a state of blissful content. He had died, not in the land of his enemies, but, thanks to the munificence of Allah Almighty, in the Holy Land. There he was buried, near the tomb of the Prophet, upon whom the blessings of Allah, and the Companions of the Prophet, may Allah be pleased with them. And may Allah also be pleased with Shaikh Shamil, who was noble and courageous, an honest believer, a man beyond reproach.

Two things had made Daghestan stand in the way of the Russians: first, the great mountains that were everywhere and, secondly, the nature of its people, dauntless horsemen who suffered the miseries of war for years upon years. If the Russians had failed to occupy Gunib and take Shaikh Shamil captive, Allah alone knows how long the Daghestanis would have continued to fight, to sacrifice themselves and to strive for the sake of their nation, their religion and their honour.

'Here Grandfather excused himself. "This evening's tale, my children, has made me very tired. I feel a great sadness whenever I tell it. And so I will bid you an early good night and I promise you that tomorrow's tale will be more cheerful, if Allah wills."'

19

Mother said, 'The next evening, when Grandfather started to speak, his voice was subdued but his face was lit up...'

A few months after the Russians occupied Daghestan I met during the Pilgrimage a couple of Circassians. The war had not yet reached their lands and they told me that they would be able to take me with them to Daghestan, and specifically to the town of Shirwan.

The war had spread to the rest of the Caucasus mountains and people were everywhere resisting the Russians, but not with the peerless steadfastness of the Daghestanis over many years. The Russians made colossal efforts and eventually succeeded in taking town after town in these distant Caucasian lands.

I arranged with these two young Circassian pilgrims that we would go back to Damascus together after the Pilgrimage. We would stay there for a few days while I got my things ready. We would then go on to Beirut, take a steamer to Turkey and travel overland to Daghestan. My travelling companions well knew the ways through those mountain paths and I had confidence in them. I promised them that I would reward them handsomely once we reached the town of Shakki and that I would be responsible for the expenses of the entire journey.

The voyage from Beirut to Turkey would have been very agreeable if there had been nothing on my mind. But I had a number of anxieties preoccupying me and did not really enjoy it at all.

What worried me most was that I would reach Shakki after all these years – thirty-five in all – of yearning to go back there only to find that mother was no longer alive. I would then have to be satisfied with a visit to her grave and undertake the difficult return journey to Damascus disappointed and disheartened. But something deep inside me spoke and reassured me whenever I became too morbidly pessimistic and radiated a blazing sensation of hope in my soul.

We reached Turkey and stayed one night. I had long wanted to visit this fair land, especially Constantinople, but I decided to put off exploring it until my return journey. My companions took possession of the two horses they had left in the care of a horse-dealer. I hired a third horse for which I paid the full price on the understanding that I would hand it back to the dealer on my return minus the cost of hiring it.

We bought sufficient provisions, mounted our horses and headed for Daghestan.

We encountered no problems on the mountainous roads on which there were very few other travellers. From time to time we would see a traveller on horseback or on foot. We would exchange greetings and then continue on our separate ways. Or we would see herdsmen with their flocks, from whom we would buy milk which was intensely delicious and reminded me of my happy childhood.

We finally reached Shakki. I bade farewell to my companions and paid them. They thanked me profusely and disappeared.

Here I was then, in Shakki, my cherished birthplace. My golden dream was now being realized. By Allah, how I hoped that the town would be prosperous and in good shape. The features of the town had not changed, though everything looked a little older. Some houses were in ruins, probably the consequence of the war. But why did the town have the appearance of being deserted? There were a few Russian soldiers strutting around. The sight of them made me feel furious. It must be that after their defeat people preferred to stay indoors after the day's labours. Here was the town square and here was the mosque. Just by the mosque was a narrow alleyway. My mother's father used to live in the first house in this alley and next door was our house, the house my brothers had sold when they moved to Damascus.

I dismounted and went up to the door of my grandfather's house. My heart was pounding so furiously that I could actually hear it beating. Never in all my life had I been in such a state of nervous anxiety as at the moment when I raised my hand to knock at the door. I held back from knocking fearing lest one of my aunts or uncles emerge with bad news about Mother.

I finally plucked up enough courage and knocked at the door. It was opened by a young woman in a white head-dress. It was Mother! But had Mother evaded the ravages of age? I stood before her, struck dumb, too embarrassed to speak. But, no, no. This was not Mother. If it had been her she would have known me at once.

The woman spoke, 'Who are you and what do you want?'

'I've come to enquire about the house of Umm Salih.' My heart pounded away again.

'Where have you come from?'

'I've come from Damascus.'

She examined me closely and then said, 'What do you want from Umm Salih?'

'I . . . I want nothing from her. I just want her, just her.'

'Is your name Salih?'

'How did you know that?'

'I know that because you're my brother.'

'Then you are my sister.'

We fell into each other's arms and wept.

'Take me to Mother, take me to her.'

'Keep your voice down. I'm afraid Mother will hear you.'

'Why should I keep my voice down? Let me go to her.' And I nearly pushed her aside.

'What can I say to you, brother?' she said in gentle tones. 'Our mother has lost her sight.'

'Mother? Blind?' I slapped my forehead so hard that I all but knocked myself out. I nearly fell over.

Then Mother's dulcet throaty voice reached me from within, 'Who are you talking to, Khadija?' she said.

For a moment Khadija said nothing. She then dashed inside. I followed her on tiptoe.

Mother was sitting on a mattress in the middle of that room where we used to spend winter evenings.

I pulled myself together as far as I could and remained silent. I looked at her, my heart beating furiously. In spite of a few gentle wrinkles around her mouth and eyes, her face was still kind and beautiful. Her black hair had turned grey, and her wide eyes were staring into space, expressionless.

Those radiant eyes, so precious to my memory, had lost their sparkle. I began to weep in torrents.

Mother gazed into the emptiness. 'Why do you not tell me, girl,' she said, 'with whom you have been talking?'

'There was a man at the door asking after you.'

'A man asking after me? What did he want of me?'

'He said all he wanted was Umm Salih.'

'Where has this man come from?'

'He says he has come from Damascus.

'Let him come in, Khadija. This is my son, Salih. Come here, Salih, come here, my boy, to the bosom of your sightless mother. Did you have to wait until I went blind from grief and longing for you before you came back to see me?'

I ran forward and fell on my knees before her. I kissed her hands and feet and buried my head in her bosom. We were all in tears.

Then Mother, amid her sobs, said, 'How I have longed to see your fair face, my son,' and she proceeded to feel my face with her hands. 'You've grown a beard. Is it jet-black as your hair used to be?'

'It's turned grey, mother.'

'No. No. I cannot believe that you have gone grey. You're still young, my son.'

'When I left Daghestan, mother, I was only ten years years old. Thirty-five years have gone by since then. Is it really surprising that your son's hair has turned grey?'

'In my mind you are still young. It is not possible for me to picture you as a man of forty-five. Have you not married? How many children do you have?'

'I was late in getting married. I insisted on getting married only to a woman who looked like my mother.'

'And did you find a girl who looked like your mother?'

'I did. She really is like you. But she is not as beautiful as you are. You, Mother, are the most beautiful woman in the world.'

She shook her head and said what was past was past, and then asked, 'What is your wife's name? Is she from Damascus? How many children has she given you?'

'Her name is Zainab. She's Georgian and very sweet. You will love her dearly, Mother, when you get to know her. She has given me one son whom I have named Najib. He is now fifteen years old.'

'Why have you had only one son, my boy?'

'It was the will of Allah, mother.'

'Grandfather then said, as we brushed away our tears, "There's no harm in your shedding a tear with your grandfather, for I shed many a tear that day." He then went on...'

I then asked Mother about her brothers and sisters

and she told me what had happened to each one of them. The whole family, in the past so tightly bound together, was now dispersed. Mother's older brother had been dead for ten years. The next brother had died a martyr's death in the revolt. Two younger brothers and their families had migrated with her eldest sister to Turkey, and two younger sisters had moved with their families to Iran.

'Emigration is the biggest mistake the Daghestanis have committed,' Mother said. 'I tried to dissuade your uncles and aunts from going away but failed. Do we have to abandon our land and our homes to the invader and then run away? The Russians have taken over houses abandoned by their owners. They either occupy them or destroy them and build in their place quarters for their soldiers. I have decided to live in this house with Khadija so that if my brothers ever come back they will find the house in good condition. Your brother, Sa'id, is still in his father's house, looking after that as well. As for Khadija, your sister, her husband was killed in the revolt when he was yet a bridegroom, just one month after the marriage. That was three years ago. She has refused to marry again in spite of many offers.'

My sister brushed away her tears and I knew that her grief was not yet over.

'But how can we have forgotten, Khadija, to let your brother, Sa'id, know that Salih is here,' Mother went on. 'He will be very cross with us. Go and tell him, girl.'

Khadija said that it was the time that he usually called. Hardly had she said this than I heard the sound of a key turning in the lock. My brother Sa'id came in, a fine looking young man, tall and spare, dressed in elegant Daghestani dress. He looked at me in astonishment as he saw me sitting comfortably between his mother and sister.

'Do you know who this is, Sa'id?' Mother asked. 'He's your brother, Salih.'

Sa'id then sprang at me and we embraced and kissed each other.

I then heard Mother muttering sadly, 'If only I had eyes to see my sons embracing each other. I feel as if a knife is turning in my heart.'

How I loved my brother and sister. I felt as if I had been brought up with them. It did not seem possible we had known each other for no more than an hour or so.

'Khadija, my dear,' said Mother, 'What are you going to prepare for dinner? I wish I could help you.'

'Don't worry yourself, Mother. I'll get everything ready myself.'

She then went and whispered something to her brother which I did not hear. Sa'id left the house and was absent for a little while. When he came back he handed something to his sister who took it into the kitchen. I realized that he had bought food to cook. I felt embarrassed. Was I being treated as a guest, a stranger, and were they preparing a feast in my honour? I would prefer them to have prepared a meal with whatever was already available in the house. I would not let this happen again. But there was no point in raising objections this time.

Sa'id came up to me.

'Would you like to have a wash and get out of your travelling clothes?' he asked. 'I can let you have some of my clothes.'

'I don't want to give you any trouble. I do have some spare clothes. Where's my saddle-bag?'

'Khadija has put it in the room you'll be sleeping in.'

'Which room is that? I can still remember the layout of the house.'

'The end room, with the windows overlooking the street.'

'That used to be Grandfather's room. May Allah have mercy on him.'

'You have a very good memory, my son,' Mother said. 'You were no more than ten when you left this town.'

How my heart ached as I saw Mother talking and looking vacantly into space. Ah, Allah, I never ever wanted to witness this terrible sight. I all but died of anger at the turn of cruel fate. I sought the mercy of Allah and repented all the sins I had committed. I went up to the room assigned to me. I opened my bag, remembering that I had brought some presents. The shock of Mother's blindness had made me forget everything. I took out a towel and a loofah, a clean shirt, trousers and a kaftan, and followed my brother Sa'id. He led me to a small room next to the kitchen, its floor paved with white stones. There was a basin and a large jug, before which stood a wooden chair.

'I can't remember this room at all,' I said.

'This was built later. We turned it into a bathroom. I believe you used to take a shower in the kitchen.'

I can remember that.

Sa'id then went to fetch some warm water from the kitchen to fill the basin. I washed myself according to Islamic ritual and put on my clean, light clothes. I felt refreshed.

I performed the sunset prayers in my room and then joined the rest of the family. The table had been laid and they were all waiting for me.

I looked at the table. 'This is my favourite Daghestani dish,' I said. 'Superb boiled meat, each piece of meat on a fine bone. We used to use our hands and chew it. We would eat it with a mouthful of delicious soup made from a meat broth to which was added a dough that had been cut into small cubes. This would all be handed out to each of us, the portions large or small depending on how much we liked it. It would be served in a soup bowl to which a mixture of crushed garlic mixed with red hot pepper and some tomato or lemon juice would be added. Daghestanis never have enough of food like this. They munch at the meat and sip at the soup until the plates are completely empty. We then used to eat fresh fruit – pears and apples and sweet-smelling grapes, all of which grow in our glorious mountains and fertile plains.'

Khadija sat next to Mother, handing her pieces of meat and pouring out soup and sauce, then peeling the fruit for her. Mother ate quietly and as daintily as if she was not blind.

When we finished I said to Sa'id, 'Would you be good enough to bring in the saddle-bag, Sa'id.'

Sa'id got up and brought the bag in. The first thing I took out was a sealed bottle of water from Zamzam. I poured a little out into a glass and handed it to Mother, saying, 'In a few months' time you'll be drinking Zamzam water from the source, if Allah wills.'

'What are you saying, my son? Are you going to take me on the Pilgrimage, Salih, and me blind?'

'What has that got to do with it? It will be doubly beneficial to you. I promised Father that I would take you on the Pilgrimage and there is no question about it: I will carry out my promise.'

'Your father, may Allah have mercy on him and be good to him, asked you to do that?'

'Yes, it was on the day he told me of his divorce from you. I wept copiously that day, but he persuaded me that he had divorced you out of love for you. He had become a helpless old man, unsuitable for a beautiful girl like you. I promised him that I would come to Daghestan when I had grown up and could afford it. I would take you on the Pilgrimage. But circumstances, Mother, kept obliging me to postpone coming. It has not been possible until this year. I will also take Sa'id and Khadija.'

'Oh, my son, if only I could see, my happiness would then be complete.'

We all had lumps in our throats. I wanted to change the subject and so brought out the presents.

'This Indian silk cloth is all for you, Mother, and this one with bright colours is for my sister Khadija. This *abaya* of soft wool with embroidered fringes of gold and silver thread is for you, Sa'id. And these prayer-beads are for you to give to whomever you wish – family or friends. These dates and this incense, these carnelian rings, the toothbrushes, the coffee – are for you all.'

They were delighted with the presents and even more delighted at my undertaking to accompany them on the Pilgrimage. They would see Constantinople, Beirut and Damascus. They had never left Daghestan or indeed Shakki. Khadija described the presents and their colours to Mother.

Sa'id took the opportunity of their preoccupation with the presents to take me aside. 'I have heard,' he said, 'that there is a famous skilled Russian eye surgeon now in Daghestan. They say he has performed wonders. A blind man whom I know well went to him. This man had been without his sight for over three years, just like Mother. The surgeon performed an operation on him and his sight was restored just as it had been before.'

'You have known this and kept silent until now? Why didn't you take Mother to him as soon as you heard about him?'

He blushed and there were tears in his eyes. He was too embarrassed to reply and I realized that he had been unable to afford either the expense of the journey or the fee to the surgeon for the operation. I was both distressed and angry with myself. I had enough money and Mother had been a prisoner of darkness for three whole years because she did not have enough money for the operation. 'Let's take Mother to him tomorrow morning,' I said.

'The town he is in is a whole day's journey from here.'

'We'll go and see him even if it is at the end of the world. But do you think the operation will be successful?'

'They say he examines every patient thoroughly, and if there is any hope of a cure, he carries out the operation. If not he excuses himself.'

'Say nothing to Mother or Khadija about this,' I said. 'We'll surprise them in the morning.'

'Here,' Mother said, 'Grandfather looked at his watch and got up, saying, "Well, well, it's almost midnight. We've been talking away quite unaware of how time has been flying.'

'We said, "Tell us just one thing, Grandfather, just one word. Was your mother's operation successful?"

'He said as he made his way towards the door, "That's not allowed in stories. Tomorrow you will know the answer."'

20

Mother said, 'The next evening we were waiting impatiently for Grandfather to resume his tale. When the time came and Grandfather took his usual seat among us, his face was bright and a smile played upon his face. We took this as a good sign as he began...'

I did not sleep at all that night, even though I was drained and exhausted after the travel and the terrible unexpected shock. I found I was talking to myself,

'How magnificent it would be if the operation is successful. What will I be able to do if a miracle happens and Mother's sight is restored?' I made a solemn vow. 'I will sacrifice ten sheep and distribute the meat to the poor of Shakki if the operation succeeds.'

The night seemed to go on for ever. At the first glimmer of dawn I got up quietly to avoid disturbing the others. I performed my ritual ablutions, prayed and brought out my copy of the Qur'an and read it to myself. Whenever I completed a *sura* I made two prostrations. I faced my Lord and prayed with all my heart that He bestow His grace on me and give Mother back her sight.

A little later Mother woke up. I heard her calling for Khadija who hurried to her to help her from her room to wash and perform the dawn prayer. After I heard her completing her prayers I went to her and bade her good morning.

'I've missed you, Mother. The night has been very long.'

'Come and sit down beside me. I can't really believe that you are here with us until I can touch you with my hands. If I don't I shall think I am having a beautiful dream.' Sa'id came in and greeted us. I whispered to him, 'Don't say a word about the doctor until we have had breakfast.'

The sun rose. Khadija was in the kitchen getting breakfast ready. We Daghestanis love our breakfast. We start working early and go back to our houses early to relax and welcome visitors. When we have had our share of rest we are then ready to dance and to sing, to play games and swap jokes and recite poetry until the middle of the night.

After breakfast Sa'id and I sat on either side of Mother. I opened the subject.

'Listen, Mother. We have a very important surprise for you.'

'Can there be any surprise more wonderful than your coming here?'

'Yes, there can. This is a surprise we have all dreamt about. Sa'id says that he has heard of a skilled Russian eye surgeon here in Daghestan, not far from here. He has been able to restore the sight of some people who had been blind. What do you think of the idea of our going today to see him to see if he can treat you?'

Mother laughed scornfully. 'Do you believe everything that is told you, my son? Is it possible that your mother's sight can come back to her after she has spent three years in utter darkness?'

'Is that not up to Allah Almighty?'

'Yes, of course it is up to Allah, but listen to me – spend your money more profitably.'

'Is there anything in the world more profitable than having your sight restored to you?'

'I have seen with my own two eyes, Mother,' said Sa'id, 'a man from this town of ours who was blind. He went to this surgeon who carried out a simple operation on him. As a result of that he can now see – and he had been blind for more than three years, the same length of time as yourself.'

'Is this true what you say, my son? Put your trust in Allah. I rely upon Him and derive solace from Him.' Mother said this in Arabic, which she knew well, having learnt to read and write it from father.

Khadija was following what we were saying. She was also muttering prayers.

'Get mother dressed,' I said, 'and pack some night clothes. Do you have enough food in the house for us?'

'I have already prepared enough food for the journey,' said Sa'id. 'There's boiled eggs, cheese, some fruit and some water.'

'That's ample,' I said. I then asked him, 'Does the doctor have someone who knows both Russian and also our language?'

'We don't need an interpreter. I know Russian.'

'And when did you learn Russian, you clever fellow?'

'When I was young. My father – may Allah have mercy on his soul – used to tell us that we had to learn the language of our enemy so that they would not be able to outsmart us. In this town there used to be people who could teach Russian to anyone who wanted to learn it. My knowledge of Russian has helped me a great deal since the occupation. They respect somebody who knows their language.'

'I'll come with you to make sure Mother is comfortable,' Khadija said.

'We mustn't leave the house empty,' said Sa'id.

'You must stay, and I'll ask the neighbours to send a daughter to stay overnight with you and keep you company. I'll also ask a friend to stay in the other house while I'm away. Russians take over houses as soon as there's nobody in them.'

Khadija held her tongue. I said to her, 'I don't like to see you so downcast. I prefer to see you always smiling. It'll only be three or four nights before we are back and we'll be back, with Mother's sight restored to her, if Allah wills it.'

She stretched her hands upward and said, 'Lord above.'

'I'll go and get a horse-cab,' Sa'id said. 'It can wait in the square just at the opening to our alleyway.' Sa'id went out and was back a few minutes later, telling us that a horse-cab was ready.

'I've forgotten that I left my horse with you. What news is there of it?'

Sa'id smiled and said, 'I wish you would continue to forget that you had left a horse with us. Don't worry about it. I've left it with one of my friends to look after.'

'If you really like the horse, then please take it as a present from me.'

Sa'id came and kissed my hand. 'That's very generous of you, brother,' he said. 'When my father died – and that's ten years ago – his horse was killed at the same time. Ever since then it has been my ambition to own a horse.'

'Now you do. It's all yours.'

205

We climbed into the cab. Mother and I sat on one side and Sa'id on the seat opposite.

The four young horses set off at a brisk pace, drawing the cab behind them. The mountain road was rough and steep. It was a fine spring morning, but when I am worried about something I am not able to enjoy such things. We sat in silence and heard only the sound of the horses' hooves as they struck the ground, and the murmurings of Mother as she mouthed her prayers. Each of us was sunk in our own reflections. What I feared most was that an operation would not be possible. What a bitter and painful disappointment that would be, after her hopes had been so raised. What a blunder we would have made. We should have thought of some deception, taking her without her being aware that we wanted her to have treatment for her eyes. There was no doubt that her dearest wish at that time was to see my face. Allah be praised. Why do I think of the right thing only when it is too late?

Sa'id wanted to distract us, calling our attention to the colours of the huge mountains and to the overhanging rocks which had ivy and flowers clinging to them. We humoured him a little and relapsed into silence.

After four hours we arrived at a small village. The driver stopped the cab. 'We must take a break here for one hour at least,' he announced. 'The climb through the mountains has exhausted the horses. I've got to feed them and give them something to drink and let them have a rest. You too can have a rest at the *khan* here. It is set up as somewhere for travellers to break their journey.'

The driver took us to the *khan* where we received a warm welcome. The owner gave us some seats covered with lambskin and a jug full of cold water collected from one of the nearby purling streams. Sa'id brought the provisions out but none of us had any appetite. We each had a few small mouthfuls and gave what was left over to the driver.

It was time to get back on the road. We returned to the cab and were soon on our way again. The road now went downhill, but the ascent had been gentler than the descent into the valley far below. We were all alarmed, fearing that the cab would plunge us into the abyss below. Even my sightless mother who was unable to appreciate the steepness of the downward road was alarmed. I heard her saying every now and then, 'Merciful Allah, have mercy on us, dear Lord.' When we reached the foot of the mountain we proceeded on level ground and then after a couple of hours and just before sunset we reached the small town where the surgeon lived.

'What do you say to the idea of our going straightaway to the surgeon?' I said to Sa'id. 'That way we can sleep comfortably tonight.'

'I was about to make the same suggestion, but you beat me to it.'

He then asked passers-by about the surgeon's clinic until he found somebody who showed us the way there. It was not far way. The clinic was in a small country house. The surgeon had assigned one room to examining patients, one to operations and the third to being a waiting-room.

A Russian — perhaps the doctor's assistant — received us. Sa'id spoke to him and we were shown into the waiting-room. We were pleased to see that there was nobody else there. Shortly afterwards the surgeon came in and greeted us very courteously. I liked the man as soon as I set eyes on him and noted that his glance embraced mother with a look of compassion. He at once realized that she was the patient. He took her by the hand and led her to the examination room and beckoned to us to follow. He sat mother down on a chair in front of him and started asking her some questions. Sa'id interpreted. The surgeon then put a ophthalmo-scope over one of his eyes. His assistant lit a torch and held it to mother's eyes. The surgeon pulled up her eyelids and examined her pupils with the ophthalmoscope He asked Mother to look up, then down and then to either side. He then examined the other eye. When he had finished he raised his ophthalmoscope and patted Mother's shoulder. He turned to Sa'id and said, 'Tell your excellent mother that her eyes are sound. It's nothing but a cataract. The operation is simple. There's no need to worry. I'll carry out the operation in the morning.

Then after three days I'll remove the bandages and she will be able to see as well as she did before.'

'Grandfather interrupted his tale here,' Mother said.

"'Do you know what I did, youngsters?' he asked us. "I took the surgeon's hand and started to kiss it. He muttered something in Russian and took his hand away."'

That moment was the happiest moment in my whole life. I turned to Mother to congratulate her and found she had half-fainted from an excess of joy. The doctor asked his assistant for a glass of water and added a few drops of medicine for her to take to revive her spirits. He put the glass to her lips. She drank it and was at once feeling better.

As she stared as usual into space with her dead eyes, she said, 'Is it true what the man is saying? Will my eyesight come back in three days' time? Will I be able to see your face, Salih?'

'If Allah wills, Mother.'

'All things are through the will of Allah. At any rate, praise be to Allah.'

The surgeon told us to come back the following day at nine o'clock. The cab was still waiting. The driver took us to a *khan* quite near the clinic. He took his fare and left us.

We had something to eat at the *khan* and spent the night there, the three of us in one room.

We woke up just as the day was beginning to dawn. Sa'id took Mother to the bathroom. She washed and said her prayers. When the sun was up the owner of the *khan* brought us some breakfast, after which we dressed for the day. It was time to go and see the surgeon. We went on foot. Mother leant on me and grasped my hand. 'I am very frightened, Salih.'

'I know you to be bold and full of courage. What is there to worry about?'

'Don't you know what is happening to your mother? It's old age, my boy.'

At the clinic the surgeon was waiting for us. He took mother straight to the operating room. Sa'id and I stayed in the waiting-room. For the patient's family this was the most difficult time.

The operation was over in an hour. The surgeon came out to reassure us. With the humility of a learned man he said, 'I believe the operation has been successful. It will be better for her to stay at the clinic under observation till this evening.'

He then brought her to the waiting-room and found a bed for her. He asked Mother to lie down and stretch out on her back and try not to move. He then told us, 'I would prefer you to leave now, because I'm going to give her a sleeping pill. She will not get over the effects until shortly before sunset. You must then come and collect her, and come back again in three days' time when I can remove the bandages from her eyes.'

The next three days seemed an eternity. We stayed at the small *khan* to be with Mother.

On one occasion I tried to divert her. 'I'll tell you, Mother, about an incident that happened to me the day Father gave me the news of his divorcing you. I was very upset, very distressed, in spite of all the lovely things Father said about you. He was full of noble feelings and had the deepest affection for you. I went back to bed but couldn't get to sleep. I was sobbing so much that I felt as if I was choking. When I was sure Father was fast asleep I slipped out of the room and went into the street. I sat down on a boulder by a wall and looked up to the sky and bemoaned my fate to my Lord. There were some flimsy clouds in the sky and the moon sent out pale rays. Then suddenly I saw your face as if it was being radiated from one of these clouds. You were wearing a blue dress and your two long plaits hung down over your breast. You seemed to come nearer me and then went away. As you came nearer me I looked at you in amazement and stretched out my hand, hoping to touch you and clasp you to me. Then you disappeared.'

'When did all this take place, my son?' asked Mother.

'It was shortly before dawn on the night before 'Arafat in the year your husband went on the Pilgrimage.'

'May Allah be praised. On that very night, the night before Arafat in the year my husband went on the Pilgrimage, I saw you, Salih, exactly as you saw me. I was missing you terribly. That night I felt a sense of apprehension that all but overwhelmed

211

my spirits. I left my room and went up on to the roof. I gazed up at the moon, and there I seemed to see you emerging from a cloud. You were wearing your Daghestani clothes that I so loved to see you wearing, and on your head you had your black *kalpak*. You came towards me and then withdrew and then again you approached so close that I imagined that I would be able to clasp you to my bosom. You then vanished and I could no longer see you. I was afraid that Satan had brought you before me and I was about to call out, "Say, I seek refuge in the Lord of people." And that night I was indeed wearing a blue dress.'

'And, mother, I too was reciting the verse, "Say, I seek refuge in the Lord of people." For I too feared that Satan was playing tricks with me.'

'Allah, may You be blessed, how mighty is Your power. Allah took pity on us, my son, and made possible this encounter between us, you in the Hijaz and I in Daghestan. We read the same Qur'anic verse, may the One who orders all things be praised. How merciful He is with His worshippers.'

The three days finally passed. We took Mother to the surgeon and he removed the bandages from her eyes. He put in each eye two drops. He then told Mother to close her eyes tight for a moment and then open them.

When she opened her eyes she cried out, 'I can see, my sons. I swear to you that I can see.' She looked around her and her gaze fell on me. She sighed deeply. 'You – you have got older, Salih, my son,' she said. 'Come and let me kiss you now.'

We all wept and even the surgeon had to dab his eyes.

I looked at Sa'id. 'Shouldn't we have brought a present for this excellent surgeon who has restored our mother's sight?' I said.

'I've brought with me the cloak you gave me. Would that do?'

'May Allah give you long life. Run to the *khan* and bring it here at once. I will get you a a better one.'

I then paid the surgeon his fee and gave a tip to his assistant. Sa'id was soon back. I took the cloak and presented it to the surgeon. He accepted it with thanks, then unfolded it and put it over his shoulders. He was very pleased with it and asked me which country it had come from.

'It is from a land far away,' I said. 'It is from Mecca.'

'It is then from a Holy Land.'

'Yes, it is from our Holy Land.'

'I will take great care of it,' he said with gentle courtesy.

'Grandfather got up and said, "We will stop at this point. Tomorrow if Allah wills, we will carry on the story."

'We all said in unison, "This has been the best of bedtime stories, Grandfather."'

21

Mother said, 'Grandfather resumed the tale with the words...'

The return journey was much less stressful, because the driver brought us back by a route that was easier though longer.

Mother talked and talked, full of joy and happiness. 'Just look how wonderful the blue sky is! How splendid these great mountains! Look, Salih, the colour of this mountain is slightly red, that one is slightly blue and the one over there dark greyish. This green valley is so beautiful. And the birds flying and twittering and these butterflies fluttering before us. I have never seen such beauty. I never appreciated it all until I lost the power of sight. Now that Allah has been bountiful to us and restored my sight I have learnt how to appreciate this gift of His. How kind You are, Allah.'

And so it was with one novelty after another until we reached a *khan* and the driver stopped to rest the horses. We ate what we could and continued our journey.

We reached our house shortly before sunset. Khadija and her friends were standing at the door waiting for us. As soon as Khadija saw Mother walking by herself unaided, she ran up to her, hugged her and kissed her, tears pouring down her cheeks. She then went back into the house and danced and sang as if she had gone crazy with happiness.

These were unforgettable days for they were indeed the happiest days of my life.

After a magnificent dinner that Khadija had prepared for us, I said to Sa'id, 'I want to say my dawn prayers tomorrow in the mosque.'

'I'll come and collect you before the call to prayer, and we can go together.'

That night I fell asleep as soon as I closed my eyes. It was the first time I had a good night's sleep in Daghestan.

At the first glimmer of dawn Sa'id called.

'Do you know what I want to do after prayers?' I said.

'Praise be to Allah Who knows whatever is in your mind.'

'I wish to fulfil a vow I have made.'

'And what, I wonder, is that vow?'

'I have made a vow to myself to sacrifice ten rams and to distribute them to the poor of Shakki, since Allah has blessed us and cured Mother of her blindness. Straight after prayers we will go to the souk to buy the rams before the shepherds take them out to the pasture. We will take them to the imam of the mosque and entrust him with the task of distribution. He is the man who knows best all the people of Shakki.'

'May Allah grant you a life that is long, brother. You are most generous.'

When I presented the rams to the imam he said, 'Allah accepts your vow, my son, and will give you your reward. The poor of the town are in dire need after the hardships of the war we have gone through. They will be ready for a generous gift like this.'

It was a Daghestani custom to compose songs when important, strange or unusual events took place. The lads and young men would sing at their evening gatherings or on other occasions. Rarely was the identity known of the author of these songs that recorded the history of the people and were handed down the generations. One song originated on the occasion of Mother's regaining her sight. The song told of the son who returned to his mother after a long absence and found her blind. Just as Joseph cured the blindness of his father so the son who had long been away cured his mother. Therefore let us sing and sing.

Visitors continued to make calls on us all day and for part of the night, coming to congratulate Mother on her recovery. They came to sing and dance for her, expressing their happiness.

After two weeks I announced to my brother and sister, 'The time has come for us to get ready to travel to Damascus.'

Sa'id set about organizing things. He found from among neighbours and his friends people who were ready to live in the two houses while we were all away, and somebody else to look after the horse as well, however long we might be gone.

We packed and got ready, and set off on the road to Turkey. I will not spend a lot of time on this journey, my children. You already know about travel in these parts. We spent four days in Constantinople. They were enormously impressed when they saw that magnificent city. It exceeded whatever expectations they had, these people who had never before left Shakki, except for trips to other villages or visits to neighbouring towns. They were amazed and delighted on seeing the Bosphorus, the outstanding mosques, the great palaces and the elegance of the people on the streets. They asked me about everything.

These five days in Constantinople passed

quickly; they were happy days. We then boarded a steamer that ploughed through the waves to Beirut. It was a glorious cruise. There was a full moon and we would spend part of the night on deck savouring the sight of the sea as it glittered in the moonlight.

'Sometimes I imagine I am dreaming,' Khadija said. 'I have to pinch myself to make sure that I am not asleep.'

Sa'id enjoyed wandering around the ship and there was no part of it that he did not see. I sat next to Mother and we would talk about those happy days before I moved from Daghestan and about how we missed each other during those years of separation.

What gave me greatest satisfaction, my children, was to be able to give pleasure to others. It was particularly gratifying when those others were people whom I loved most and who were nearest to me.

We reached Beirut and stayed there for one day and one night. But after Constantinople, my mother and my brother and sister could care for no other city.

We then took a diligence – a large vehicle with a lot of seats drawn by several horses – and in twelve hours we were in Damascus. From the city centre a cab took us to the house in Salihiya.

I had been sorely missing my son and my wife, my house and all my family. Life had been so full of incident that I was pining to see them. I did not knock at the door. Instead I took my key from my pocket, opened the door and took my guests inside. I stood in the middle of the courtyard and called out at the top of my voice, 'Zainab, Najib, come and meet my mother, and my brother and sister.'

It was a rapturous meeting, with kisses, embraces and tears of joyfulness. Mother fell in love with my wife and son. 'I praise Allah with all my heart and soul,' she said, 'for He has given me the blessing of being cured of my blindness so that I am able to enjoy seeing those whom I love.'

I then took them on a tour of all the house which gave them much pleasure.

'I never imagined that a great river could flow through a house, my son,' said Mother. 'The garden and the fountain are wonderful.'

Next morning I sent my son, Najib, to the house at Bab al-Barid to tell the family there that my own family had arrived. They all came – including the girls and the women – to welcome my own relations.

The women then organized feasts in honour of the guests. It pleased Mother no end to meet everybody who came to see her. I insisted on my elder sister, Umm Muhammad, staying with us so she and Mother could enjoy things together, for my wife and son could speak the language of Daghestan only with great difficulty. When I went off to work there was now Umm Muhammad who could take on the role of interpreter. Mother and my brother and sister stayed in Damascus for a whole month before the season of the Pilgrimage. I took them to the Umayyad Mosque, to the souks and other sights of Damascus, to the gardens and cafés and to the fair suburbs. As the Pilgrimage time approached we made our preparations for the journey. I sought permission from the Pasha to take mother with me on the leading camel. He gave his consent, I am happy to say, to my request. I also rented a camel especially for my brother and sister.

Throughout the whole period of the Pilgrimage I remained at Mother's side, in other words, for four whole months. I was separated from her only when I had to be on duty. I looked after her myself, especially when she performed the prescribed rites of the Pilgrimage.

As the time to go back to Damascus approached I took my family to the souk to buy presents they wanted to take back to Daghestan.

My spirit enjoyed a feeling of total bliss. I did not believe, my children, that there was any happiness equal to this sense of spiritual bliss.

On our return to Damascus, when we were in the lead caravan, I said to Mother, 'To be apart from you is very hard, Mother. I have become used to seeing you and talking to you every day. What do you think of the idea of staying on with me in Damascus? You and Khadija and Sa'id can live in the outer house which you like so much.'

She looked at me disapprovingly.

'Do you want me to move away from my own country?' she said reproachfully. 'To leave the land and the house of my father and the house of my husband to the hands of the enemy? To do for them just what they want? Should I who have been so critical of those who have left their country leave my country? No, a thousand times no, Salih. I was expecting you to return to your country, not you to invite me to quit it.'

'You're absolutely right, Mother, most wonderful Mother. I cannot hide from you the fact that I thought of returning to my country when the revolt in Daghestan was at its climax, when Shaikh Shamil was achieving victory after victory. I said to myself that if the revolt succeeded I would resign my post and give up my house and go back to Daghestan. If I were to live there for a long time on next to nothing I would be able to build up my life anew. But the revolt collapsed and as I own not a single square metre of land in my own country I felt obliged to be prudent. And I have no skills on which I would be able to earn enough to live. There would be no job available to me. The occupying forces have taken all the important positions and the minor posts have been allocated to their supporters. Because of all this I decided not to come home.'

'I think you were partly right in what you thought, but how can you be sure there won't be another revolt, one that will spread to the whole of the Caucasus, and bring us victory.'

'Do we have another leader who could unite the people of all the Caucasus, just as Shaikh Shamil united the whole of Daghestan?'

'That leader will come, just as Shaikh Shamil came.'

'This is very difficult to achieve.'

'Why should it be difficult to achieve? Where did Shaikh Shamil come from? He came from the loins of a Daghestani woman. There are still women, and, praise be to Allah, throughout the whole of the Caucasus there are women who are bearing and giving birth to sons. It is not at all improbable that from among these sons there will emerge one who will in the course of time become a leader who will unite us in a way that was beyond the capacity of Shaikh Shamil.'

'You are very optimistic, Mother dear.'

'Isn't optimism better than despair? Optimism, my son, generally leads to victory and success. But despair brings in its train defeat and failure.'

When we reached al-'Asali, in the suburbs of Damascus, my brother Ahmad, my son Najib and my nephews Muhammad and Mustafa were there to welcome us. They had come in a cab which then took us to the house at Salihiya. There we found all the women of the family awaiting us, greeting us with ululations, as is the custom when Damascenes welcome returning pilgrims. This made Mother very happy.

A week after our return Mother said as we were having breakfast in the garden by the river and waterwheels, 'The time has come, Salih, for us to go home.'

'Why are you in such a hurry, Mother?' I said with a hint of reproach. 'Have you had enough of us?'

'May Allah pardon you, Salih, can a mother ever have enough of her son? These six months that I've spent with you have been the happiest in all my life. For the rest of my life I will call on you every night and pray that Allah look after your needs and bestow upon you and upon your family health and happiness. Is it not enough that, thanks to you, I am cured of blindness? But there can be no question about our returning home. We have been away for a long time, away from those friends and neighbours who are taking care of our homes and looking after our interests during this prolonged absence. Your brother, Sa'id, too, has been away from his work on the land. I have decided that, if Allah wills, we should set off in one week's time.'

I observed that Mother had acquired many of Father's characteristics. Once her mind was made up she would not go back on her word. I had to yield to her wishes, however reluctantly.

'As you wish, Mother,' I said. 'I will arrange for someone to book a place for you on a steamer on whatever day you wish.'

'I have one request to make of you, Salih.'

'Give me your orders, Mother.'

'It is my hope that you come and visit us in Daghestan whenever it is possible.'

'Why not, Mother? This is just what I was thinking myself, but on the condition that sometimes you come back with me to Damascus and stay for as long as you wish.'

'As you like, my son.'

One week later I went with Mother, Khadija and Sa'id to Beirut in a diligence to say goodbye to them. We stayed overnight in Beirut and they set sail the following morning.

I stood on the jetty gazing at the steamer as it went farther and farther away. I remained fixed to the spot unable to move until it was completely out of sight. I felt at that moment that something very precious had been taken away from my soul and I realized that it was a final farewell.

My premonition turned out to be true. One year later one of the migrants from the Caucasus brought me the news of mother's death.

I was utterly distraught. My only consolation was that she had departed from this world approving of me in every way.